Libby was in trouble...

Bile rose in Axel's throat. He hurdled all six stairs that led to the roof and into the spring sunshine.

Libby hung off the roof ledge of the next building, trying to swing her legs over the ledge, but that was far too risky. She could lose her grasp at any moment.

Axel hollered, "Stop! Stop now! Just focus on hanging on or you'll risk plummeting." His pulse thundered in his ears. Her grasp was not solid. How long had she been holding on for dear life?

"Axel! I—I don't know how much longer I've got."

Libby's frantic and petrified words turned his blood ice-cold.

If she fell, Libby would be dead.

For all he knew, the killer was on his way up to the rooftop next door to kick her off the ledge she hung from.

Without another thought, Axel sprinted the ten feet and sprang off the ledge, clearing the building and landing on the next rooftop, falling and rolling. He scrambled to his feet when she began to shriek.

"Axel! I'm losing it! I'm losing my grip!"

Jessica R. Patch lives in the Mid-South, where she pens inspirational contemporary romance and romantic suspense novels. When she's not hunched over her laptop or going on adventurous trips with willing friends in the name of research, you can find her watching way too much Netflix with her family and collecting recipes for amazing dishes she'll probably never cook. To learn more about Jessica, please visit her at jessicarpatch.com.

Books by Jessica R. Patch

Love Inspired Suspense

Elite Protectors

Attempted Mountain Abduction
A Killer in Texas

Texas Crime Scene Cleaners

Crime Scene Conspiracy
Cold Case Target
Deadly Christmas Inheritance

Quantico Profilers

Texas Cold Case Threat
Cold Case Killer Profile
Texas Smoke Screen

Love Inspired Trade

Her Darkest Secret
A Cry in the Dark
The Garden Girls
The Other Sister

Visit the Author Profile page at LoveInspired.com for more titles.

A KILLER IN TEXAS

JESSICA R. PATCH

If you purchased this book without a cover you should be aware that this book is stolen property. It was reported as "unsold and destroyed" to the publisher, and neither the author nor the publisher has received any payment for this "stripped book."

LOVE INSPIRED® SUSPENSE
INSPIRATIONAL ROMANCE

ISBN-13: 978-1-335-90645-8

A Killer in Texas

Copyright © 2025 by Jessica R. Patch

All rights reserved. No part of this book may be used or reproduced in any manner whatsoever without written permission.

Without limiting the exclusive rights of any author, contributor or the publisher of this publication, any unauthorized use of this publication to train generative artificial intelligence (AI) technologies is expressly prohibited. Harlequin also exercises their rights under Article 4(3) of the Digital Single Market Directive 2019/790 and expressly reserves this publication from the text and data mining exception.

This is a work of fiction. Names, characters, places and incidents are either the product of the author's imagination or are used fictitiously. Any resemblance to actual persons, living or dead, businesses, companies, events or locales is entirely coincidental.

For questions and comments about the quality of this book, please contact us at CustomerService@Harlequin.com.

® is a trademark of Harlequin Enterprises ULC.

Love Inspired
22 Adelaide St. West, 41st Floor
Toronto, Ontario M5H 4E3, Canada
www.LoveInspired.com

HarperCollins Publishers
Macken House, 39/40 Mayor Street Upper,
Dublin 1, D01 C9W8, Ireland
www.HarperCollins.com

Printed in U.S.A.

There is no fear in love; but perfect love casteth out fear: because fear hath torment. He that feareth is not made perfect in love.
—*1 John* 4:18

To my son-in-love, Nathan. Thank you for the way you love our feisty daughter. I see a lot of Axel in you and the way you care for B.

ONE

How did one tell their best friend—and colleague/boss—that they were being stalked and had been for over a month?

The minute Libby Winters revealed the truth, Axel Spears would lose his marbles and handcuff her to him until they caught the skeezy lurker.

Libby glanced at Axel, her closest confidant and boss for the past four years, as he stared at Harley Coburn's family estate, a deep scowl creased into his brow and his Superman jaw ticking.

The spring Texas air hung thick and wet with impending rain, and bloated gray clouds rolled in from the east, draining the sunlight and leaving them in a foreboding atmosphere.

"I do not like this," Axel said in his native drawl. Born and bred Texan, Axel exuded cowboy and ranch life, but he was fitter than the Man of Steel and, minus the blue eyes, could totally pass for the superhero. Although he didn't have the meek and mild manners of Clark Kent. He was tough and unapologetic about his bluntness, which Libby appreciated from the start.

She'd known Axel when he worked in the FBI and he'd helped investigate the First Lady's stalker. As a former Secret Service agent, Libby had been assigned to the President, First Lady and their family, depending on the day and circumstance. When she'd left after tragic circumstances, Axel had recruited her as a protection specialist—aka bodyguard for hire—at Spears & Bow, the company that he and his partner, Archer Crow, had formed after they each had left their federal agency. She'd said yes because she liked Axel, trusted him and needed a job that was less stressful.

Axel had a way of getting under her skin, but it was also another reason she liked him so much. He could dish out and take snark. That made them a fine pair of partners, and they often did their assignments together while the other members of their team, Amber Rathbone and Bridge Spencer, paired up. Archer kept behind the scenes for reasons unknown. Only Axel had private access to Archer's deal. And he never shared it. Axel was a vault. Another admirable trait in a colleague, boss and friend.

"We're not sure if we're taking this case, so don't approach Harley Coburn as if we are. I want to feel him out myself before deciding." Axel raked a hand through his thick, inky mop of hair that had grown out from his regular military cut, and Libby spied a few streaks of silver. Who needed kryptonite when age was weakening them?

Mid-forties looked good on Axel, though, and Libby could admire him without swooning. For starters, she wasn't a swooner and if that wasn't enough, she'd boxed up her romantic heart years ago, pocketing the key. Axel had done the same.

Neither had interest in romantic relationships after they'd each lost the ones they'd loved most, and it made for an easy train to ride to becoming the best of friends. Normally, they were transparent with one another. No secrets between them. But Libby hadn't confided about her shadowy stalker to him or anyone on the team. However, she had been smart enough to file two police reports with the local PD to make sure it was on record if things escalated.

"Well, let's get it over with," Libby said, nudging Axel to walk to the front door and stop staring at the Colonial style mansion. The Coburns raised cattle in the Hill Country as well as owned a major pharmaceutical company—Coburn-Pharma. And if that wasn't enough, they had their hands in many other lucrative businesses. Their money rivaled the Rockefellers', and they had offered Spears & Bow a hefty sum to protect Harley, their son. "You okay?"

Axel's jaw twitched again. "Nope. It's bringing

up old memories. My breakfast wants to come back up."

"Gross." Libby scrunched her nose. "I can do it by myself if you'd like." She knew almost as much as Axel about The Eye case—mostly from him.

This vicious serial killer had wreaked havoc all over Texas—Dallas, El Paso, San Antonio and Austin—butchering women in their homes after having stalked them like a cat after a little helpless bird—a sparrow to be exact. He left a printed copy of "His Eye is on the Sparrow" on their chests. Axel believed it was The Eye's way of letting everyone know he'd had his eye on the victim long before he murdered them.

Axel and his special FBI task force had been on the hunt for him, and Axel had been vital to the team since he had a profiling background. And then The Eye had taken Axel's wife as the eighth victim. Axel had resigned the same day he found her dead in their bedroom after a false tip had landed him in Dallas at the time of the murder.

Since he'd left the FBI and the case, The Eye had taken four more women, bringing the total body count to twelve, with the most recent just three months ago.

Axel shook his head. "Nope. I don't believe Harley Coburn is The Eye. I see why he's a person of interest at this point, but several of his alibis, including the time of Cheryl's death, are rock solid."

When Axel had been on the hunt, Harley Coburn hadn't even been on the map. It was after Axel had left that Harley became a suspect due to his connection to multiple victims. But Axel had followed the case closely and if he didn't think the killer was Harley Coburn, then he wasn't.

Axel huffed. "The FBI and local law enforcement want to put this baby to bed, and Harley is the closest they've come to doing that. They all want a person to blame."

That may be true. "If he's the wrong man, the murders won't stop."

"I know. Keeping an eye on Harley will prove if he's the guy or not. But to be safe, I want to feel him out first. I've never had to interview this man before. I only know him on paper."

People were rarely anything like their profiles on paper.

He rang the bell and they waited.

"The media is to blame for these attempted homicides and threats on Harley Coburn," Libby said. "You'd think that they would be discreet knowing how much money and power this family wields."

"Makes for a great story though. Billionaire son questioned three different times in the past couple of months over The Eye murders. He's rich. Good-looking. Privileged. Who better to believe he's invincible? And because of his money, loved ones grieving their losses would easily believe he'd walk or pay someone off. They might even think he has powerful people in his pocket like a judge or the new governor."

Libby agreed. "So one or a few decided to take matters into their own hands and become vigilantes for justice." Harley's life had been in the spotlight for something other than work or humanitarian efforts in the past couple of months. Someone had made death threats and even attempted murder on three separate occasions. When one of those attempts resulted in a bullet grazing Harley's shoulder, Spears & Bow were called in for their services.

"Exactly. Desperate people hurting do desperate hurtful things. I don't agree with it, but I understand the motivation behind the acts."

Libby understood it too, the thirst for justice and seeing it served, but they had no solid evidence Harley was The Eye. And even if he was, it was the law's job to serve justice and God's job eternally.

Finally, a stout woman in her mid-to late fifties wearing a maid's uniform opened the door. Cleaning people still wore those things? Libby hadn't realized. "You must be here to see Mr. Coburn Jr. Come. Come." She invited them inside with a sweep of her hand and led them through a foyer, a hearth room and out back to the screened-in porch overlooking a pool area that would make a perfect *Southern Living* cover if the day wasn't overcast and foggy. The fog rose from the pool like the setting to a horror movie.

Harley Coburn sat at a glass table with a cup of coffee and a bowl of fruit. He stood and smiled with a mouthful of teeth that had seen braces. Harley was in his late thirties, loved the sun, tennis and himself. Libby didn't need a background check to detect that instantly. Didn't make him a killer. Libby doubted she'd like the man much, but she didn't have to like a client to protect them with her life. She'd guarded the President, and his family, eight years ago, and she hadn't even voted for him. But she would have laid down her life for all of them.

And she nearly had.

"Agent Spears," Harley said as he extended his muscular arm, his Patek Philippe watch glimmering against his bronzed skin.

"No agent," Axel said, his face impassive and his voice even. He might be a bundle of nerves, but Harley Coburn would never know it. Libby barely saw it, but she knew him well enough to know his tell and his cheek pulsed.

"Sorry. Mr. Spears." His gaze slid to Libby, and he released his grip on Axel's hand and offered it to her. "I don't believe I've had the pleasure, but I've read your bio on the website."

"Libby Winters. Nice to meet you." Libby shook his firm hand and sized him up. Didn't look like a serial killer, but that was the thing about serial killers. One often had no idea they were under one's nose. Serial killers could be charming, good-looking, with above average intelligence. A person could sit next to them at church every Sunday, never knowing they had a string of bodies in their crawlspace.

"Likewise. Please, have a seat." He motioned for them to take chairs at the table. "Can Carmelita bring y'all a cup of coffee, tea, juice?"

"No, thank you," Libby said, and sat across from Axel.

"Mr. Coburn," Axel said. "We're not taking your case just yet, though I've reviewed the more recent police reports and your alibis."

"Then you know I am not The Eye." He shot him a pointed look as if the thought was absurd.

"I don't know it for certain," Axel said. "You were in the areas and even exact locations of some of the victims when they were killed, and you had relationships with more than one victim that the authorities know about. You make a good person of interest."

Harley seemed to consider that. "My family owns a pharmaceutical company, and I travel often due to that. These women were in the medical field. I can't help we were in the same circles." He tossed his hands up as if helpless. "I know I dated one of the roommates of a victim in Austin and dated one of the victims in El Paso, which does look bad. And I was friends with a victim in Dallas and saw her two days before she died. Maybe I'm being framed, as ludicrous as that sounds. I don't know anyone who would hold a grudge that long against me."

"You'd be surprised," Axel said.

Harley raised his eyebrows. "Truth is, Mr. Spears, I think the law is grasping at straws and needs a scapegoat, and I'm the best they have. I would have interviewed me three times too. I'm not an idiot. I went to Yale. But I did not murder these women...or your wife," he murmured. "And I am very sorry for that tragedy you endured. I understand if you don't want to take this case personally or at all. I'm not cleared exactly, and you have a personal stake. But I have been shot at twice and jumped once. My car has been keyed and my brick gates have been spray-painted. My mom isn't in good health and this is taking a toll on her, and my father is flat-out furious and expects me to handle it, though I don't know how."

Libby and Axel held each other's gaze. Harley was right on all accounts.

"I appreciate your condolences." Axel inhaled

deeply then studied Harley before releasing the breath in resignation. "We have some papers for you to fill out before we can proceed with protection services."

Harley's shoulders relaxed and his face softened, his blue eyes filling with moisture. "Thank you. I'll be honest, if you'd have said no, then I don't know what I'd have done. I guess I'd have flown overseas and stayed indefinitely, but I don't want to upend my life or crawl under a rock when I don't deserve to be there."

"Understood. If you plan to go about daily activities, then we have additional papers you'll need to sign," Axel said.

"But you'll take my case."

Axel dipped his chin. "We will. Libby, can you grab the papers?"

"Yeah. I left my cell in the car too." Libby stood and excused herself then made her way through the mansion and outside. She stepped from the porch into the mist and frowned. Just enough moisture to do a number on her hair, which was hard enough to tame. Naturally, her hair was curly but she took great pains to straight-iron the thick mass and pull it into a tight ponytail.

This was going to wreck all her time-consuming work. Hairs on her arm prickled, and she darted a glance through the foggy atmosphere as she made her way to their black Suburban.

She opened the passenger door and retrieved her cell phone then closed the door and opened the back passenger door to snag the paperwork for Mr. Coburn.

Scuffling on the pavement drew her attention. Before she had time to snag her weapon or make sense of anything, a black-clad figure snaked his arm around her neck. "Pretty little sparrow. I've been watching you. The sheets on your bed are so soft."

Libby's heart hiccupped and then training kicked in as she elbowed him and swept his foot out from under him, but he was spry and agile, recovering and bouncing out of her arm's reach. "See you soon, sparrow." He darted across the lawn and Libby gave chase, but the dense fog hid him and she lost him at the edge of the property. She fired a round into the woods to let him know she wasn't afraid and that she was armed.

Her chest heaved and her pulse ran at a wild and dangerous pace. Sparrow. She'd just been approached by The Eye. Libby's heart misfired as terror climbed into her throat.

How brazen a killer to show up like this? He'd been watching and waiting. He couldn't have known she would come to the SUV. He'd simply been spying and couldn't pass up the opportunity to let her know she had been on his radar and he'd been in her home, and she was his next target.

* * *

The crack of gunfire sent Axel bolting, the wrought-iron chair tumbling to the tile floor with a clatter. Harley's eyes widened. "Are they after me?"

"I don't know. Get inside. Room with no windows and do not come out until me or Libby come for you." Axel sprinted out of the pool area, through the iron gates enclosing it and into the yard toward the sound of the gunshot, but the fog created a blurry line of vision and he couldn't tell if that was Libby at the edge of the tree line or just a shadow.

"Libby!"

"Over here," she called.

Axel darted in her direction, eating up the ground until he reached her through the misty haze. Was she hurt? She looked in one piece. No wounds. No blood. His heart hammered against his ribs. "You hurt?"

"No," she said, but her ashen face revealed how shaken she was. Libby was cool and collected under pressure, and danger rarely if ever ruffled her feathers. Whatever had transpired was personal to her. In a big way. Now come to think of it, she'd been a little off the past month. Edgy. Slightly distracted.

"Tell me what went down out here."

"Perp got away into the woods. I fired a shot

into them." The rainy mist increased to a sprinkling and dotted her forehead, running down wan cheeks.

"I don't want bullet points. Expound." Was this about Harley Coburn or something else? Without details he couldn't make an informed decision concerning Coburn.

Libby's mouth pursed, then she let out a sigh. "I came out to the car to grab my phone and the paperwork when someone emerged from the fog. He grabbed me, and I made a move to release myself, but he was fast, Axel. Spry. Physically fit. Around six feet. Medium build. Might have combat training. He took off running, and I gave chase. Fired the round when he entered the woods." Her voice was clinical, running down facts, but her pulse in her neck ticked against her scar.

"What aren't you telling me?" They didn't keep secrets. They'd had in-depth conversations on the losses they'd both suffered, and neither held back emotions. Their friendship had been built on truth and transparency. But she was withholding information now. Why?

Libby kicked at the grass now dewy from rain. "It wasn't an attempt on Harley, Axel. It was directed to me. Personal."

Axel's heart stuttered. "What do you mean? Quit hemming and hawing, Libs. What aren't you revealing?"

She tossed her head back and groaned. "You're going to be mad."

He splayed in his hands in front of him. "I'm already mad. So no worries there." If she was in danger and hadn't been forthcoming, then Axel couldn't help protect her. Libby absolutely knew his fears about failing people he cared about. When The Eye had butchered Cheryl, he'd been miles away in Dallas and unable to help her. His entire world had imploded, shattered into tiny shards that embedded in his soul, jagged pieces that still ripped into him especially through his dreams at night, waking him in sweat-soaked sheets and taunting him.

He would never forget that horrific night when he'd returned home to discover her only to receive a phone call a few minutes later from The Eye—his voice masked by a modulator, giving him the play-by-play of killing his wife.

Libby surely wouldn't keep a life-threatening situation from him. Would she?

Libby licked her lips and started walking toward the Coburn estate. Axel jogged to catch up. "Libby, stop. You owe me details. Now." He didn't care that his voice sounded demanding and gruff. His best friend had been hiding something big.

She paused at the drive and swiped rain from her face. "For the past month and a half, someone has been stalking me."

His blood boiled and he balled a fist. "Define stalking," he said through gritted teeth. He seethed that someone had invaded her life and lurked around her, but the fact she'd kept it from him for a month and a half made him livid. Stalking was serious and dangerous. Most stalkers had obsessive tendencies fixating on their victims, and it often led to fatalities.

That thought terrified him, running neck and neck with his fury.

"I first felt watched when I'd come home in the evenings, then I felt it when I'd go out on errands—never during work hours. Always my personal time. I changed up my running routes and thought I might be paranoid—you know I have cause—but two weeks ago, I came home and someone had been inside my house."

"What?" Axel bellowed as a gasket blew in his brain. "Someone has been inside your home and you didn't tell the team, tell me? Did you even have the brains to call the police?"

"Yes," she said calmly, but her cheek pulsed. He was aware his tone was loud. But this was Libby. His best friend. And she was acting like a rookie. "I followed protocol, checked my home and I changed locks the next day, though I couldn't find a point of entry. I've filed two police reports."

She didn't mention a security system, though.

He'd make sure she had one installed or he'd do it himself. "Was anything missing from your home?"

Libby pinched the bridge of her nose. "I don't know. My undergarment drawer had been rifled through, and an impression had been left on my side of the bed. I always make my bed like a soldier. No creases. I noticed it immediately."

"Your side of the bed. How would he know which side you sleep on unless he's been able to see in your window at night when you sleep? Do you leave your blinds or windows open?"

"I am not under investigation here, Axel. It's possible I left blinds cracked but not open. I do not leave windows open at night. Open windows are open doors for killers. Not my first rodeo, and I have intimate knowledge and experience in stalking. I did help protect the First Lady." She pulled the collar of her dress shirt down, revealing a long pale scar across her neck.

Libby was right, but the thought of some sicko lying on her bed and going through her intimate apparel sickened him. Infuriated him. That was her private space and she'd been violated.

Libby didn't date so a former boyfriend was unlikely. Like Axel, she had tabled falling in love again after her fiancé, Lucas, was killed. Dating was pointless because it led the other person to believe things might become serious, and neither of them ever planned to do that again. That's why they worked so well as best friends. They had a line drawn. They were safe for each other. Needed a plus-one? They attended with one another. Easy. No complications or entanglements. Libby was hilarious and sarcastic with a quick wit. She had a sharp mind and loved many of the same things as Axel, like shooting ranges, boxing, horseback riding and early '90s country music. And she was a woman of faith and gave him sound counsel when he needed it.

They were the perfect friend couple. And she didn't have many other male friends. Stalkers were often personally known by their victims. "Any idea who it might be?"

"Not until just now." She swallowed hard and averted her gaze.

"Tell me it wasn't that cop you dated a few times. I will pulverize that jackwagon."

Libby smirked then gave him the stink eye. "It wasn't Clint. And that was three dates because he said he didn't want anything serious."

And he lied thinking she'd change her mind.

"This man said something to me when he put his arm around my neck." Her eyes widened, and he'd never seen her look afraid before. Concerned? Yes. Afraid? No.

"What did he say? Quit stalling," he demanded.

"He said, 'Pretty little sparrow. I've been watching you. The sheets on your bed are so soft.'" She flinched at the last statement, and Axel threw his hands up in the air, frustrated, and started pacing in the steady rain.

"The Eye. He's been in your house. Taken things." Cheryl had once mentioned that some of her lingerie had been rifled through and maybe a pair taken, but he'd chalked it up to the dryer monster that stole socks too. He never should have blown off her comment. She also told him she thought someone had been inside the house, and he'd put an alarm system in place after that since he'd been hot on the serial killer's trail.

But that night, she'd forgotten to set it. Hadn't had it long or been in the habit. The Eye had come in through the guest bedroom window knowing Axel was on a wild-goose chase in Dallas.

Now he was targeting Libby. Had he seen her with Axel? Was this his fault? They worked together but often did things outside of work. Had The Eye mistaken their friendship for romance? Was he going to try and rip her away from Axel as well? He had so many unanswered questions.

The biggest one: How was he going to protect Libby when he'd utterly failed his wife?

TWO

Axel made Harley Coburn comfortable in one of their office conference rooms. After the incident at the estate, the best thing to do was schedule a meeting with the team, and all except Archer were in town for now. Harley was at a table filling out the paperwork, a box lunch and soft drink next to him.

"We may be a while," Axel said.

Harley glanced up, the pen in his left hand. Another indicator he wasn't The Eye. The victims had been butchered and the medical examiner had concluded someone right-handed had done it. Was it possible Harley was ambidextrous? Yes. But unlikely. "It's okay. This is a lot of paperwork, and I can watch reruns of *The Office* on the comedy channel. I'm set."

"You need anything else?" Axel asked. Because they were always forthcoming with their clients, Harley had needed to know that The Eye had been on his property but not to target Harley.

He had his eye set on Libby. But it could complicate the assignment, and Harley had decisions he needed to make. As of now, he was still onboard with using their team to protect him.

"No. But…now that this serial killer has approached your own team member, doesn't it prove I'm not him? Won't this call off whoever is trying to kill me? Or am I in double danger now?"

Axel didn't believe The Eye cared about Harley, but he never ruled anything out to be safe. However, Harley could get hurt in the cross fire if Libby stayed on as his bodyguard. Maybe even if Axel stayed on. This was his fault. Guilt ate him like piranhas let loose in his gut. Libby had been targeted because of Axel. She wasn't medical personnel. Which meant The Eye had kept up with Axel and his life.

"We don't believe you're the target, and we'll do everything to keep you out of the cross fire. But you have the power to let us go if you feel unsafe."

"I've done the research. I think I have a better shot with your team, even with a serial killer stalking a team member, than if I went with another local agency with no trouble. I know how good Spears & Bow is. I don't want anyone else. I'll sign a waiver if I need to."

Now was a good time to throw an accusation at Harley and gauge his reaction. "Are you sure you're not feeling safe because you *are* The Eye with an accomplice? Therefore you know you're safe. No reason to let us go."

Axel had profiled the serial killer well before Cheryl had been killed. What he found was all the murders leading up to and including hers had the same signature. Identical with no subtle changes, indicating one person. Every killer had a signature—a unique, often psychologically motivated element of their crime that pronounced their personal need or fantasy. Unique to them alone. Even in cases where there had been duos—and they were extremely rare—the submissive had a slight differentiation from the dominant's signature, revealing they were indeed a duo.

Not so with The Eye's victims.

He would need to see the files of the victims after Cheryl's death to be sure about those. Axel had left the Bureau that day and never looked back, though he had kept up with the case on the news and his own personal investigating. But he suspected the more recent murders would reveal the same thing: One single killer.

Finding another right-handed sadist was slim to none. Two that could mimic a signature was near impossible.

"Do I look like a man who would want to share some glory with a buddy?" Harley asked. The man was rich, spoiled and top dog. If he—or his family—were to accept acclaim, it would be for their personal merit alone. No buddy system. That was part of the reason he believed Harley. He didn't fit the profile. Harley Coburn wasn't a team player.

"No. Thus the paperwork. I'll be back." He closed the door behind him and walked down the hall, the scent of strong coffee and cinnamon wafting on the air. Thunder rumbled and rain continued to pour down outside. Axel entered their main conference room; the team was assembled with coffees in hand. This whole case had him rattled, bringing up Cheryl's gruesome death and the fact he'd been powerless to rescue or save her.

Amber Rathbone, a former Memphis homicide detective, sat next to Libby on the far side of the table. A laptop was open in the middle of the table, Archer visible with a false background of mountains behind him. Archer Crow had once been a top operative with the CIA, and he made sure the Spears & Bow team had state-of-the-art spy gadgets to do their job—which often sent them around the United States and occasionally overseas. He had his reasons for privacy—or as Axel liked to call it, isolation. But it wasn't Axel's place to divulge that information to the rest of the bodyguards even if Axel disagreed with Archer's choices.

At the other end of the table was their admin assistant, Jolie Freemont. She was in her early twenties and obsessed with cold coffee. If Axel's coffee ever turned cold, that was a sure sign to dump it or find a microwave. And with all that whip and caramel and other junk, it was dessert not a drink. Jolie saluted as he entered, her strawberry blond hair pulled back in a tight bun on her neck. Green eyes met his. "Hey boss." She slurped her million-calorie excuse for a coffee and he smirked.

"How's Dave?"

Dave was Jolie's newest love—a donkey. A literal donkey she kept on her family's ranch not far from here. She'd inherited it from an uncle—the ranch not the donkey.

"He's kicking me less. I call that progress." She sipped her dessert drink.

Amber snorted. "Not the way one would want to go out. Death by donkey."

She raised her plastic cup. "I know what I'm doing. I've trained horses before."

Bridge Spencer, former FBI member for the Critical Incident Response Group, entered the room. "Sorry I'm late. I had to take Paisley to the doctor."

"Oh no. Is she okay?" Libby asked. She loved Bridge's six-month-old daughter and offered to babysit anytime he and his wife needed it.

"Ear infection. Molly told me how to treat her and I didn't listen. I should have and saved a copay, but she can't call in antibiotics yet so... She's read four different medical journals and all of Johns Hopkins's website." He chuckled. "Gotta love that mind."

Molly was Bridge and Wendy's adopted daughter, who had a photographic memory. As a former CIA operative, Wendy Dawson-Spencer would make a fabulous addition to the Spears & Bow team, but she was enjoying being at home with the girls for now.

Bridge sat opposite Libby and Amber, talking all things baby. After pouring a cup of coffee, Axel eased into the leather chair at the head of the table. "So here's where we are, Libby." He looked at her, still irked she'd kept him in the dark about a serious situation.

She pursed her lips and stared at the computer screen where Archer could see. "I'm in The Eye's sights—pardon the pun—though I didn't know it was him until today." She proceeded to tell the team about being stalked, someone being inside her home and what transpired at the Coburn estate today.

The room was quiet for a moment, then Archer spoke from the laptop's speakers. "You believe Harley is innocent then, Axel?"

Axel scowled. He never truly thought Harley

was guilty to begin with. "That's what you want to know? Libby has a serial killer after her and has been stalked without telling us. Who cares about Harley Coburn!" Axel stood as heat filled his neck and cheeks. What was wrong with these people?

"If Harley Coburn is innocent, then this determines next steps for everyone, including you, Libby." Archer's voice was steady and calm—even soft. Unlike the panic growing in Axel's chest.

"I don't think he's guilty," Axel said. "But I'm also not going to turn my back on him. Better to be overly cautious than dead." He shot Libby a withering glare, and she returned it with equal fervor. "Libby needs off this case immediately and sent to a safe house."

"Hold up!" Libby said, and jumped to her feet. "That is not fair. I am fully capable of doing my job. Would you take Bridge or Archer off the case if it were them?"

No, if he was being honest. But this wasn't Archer or Bridge. This was Libby.

She folded her arms over her chest. "That's what I thought. Amber, back me up."

Amber's mouth dropped open but she recovered quickly. "I mean she can do her job. Axel, you might be a little over the top here."

"Oh, he's being way extra," Jolie stated. Everyone was against him. "Like she can take down multiple grown men at once, I mean, if they don't put her in a chokehold first. But if she can keep from being contained, she can hold her own, and quite frankly, I think she could kick your can all over the street."

"Thank you? I think?" Libby said in a questioning tone.

Axel raised a skeptical eyebrow. "I think not. Libby couldn't take me down. I outweigh her by over a hundred pounds."

Bridge chuckled. "We could rent a boxing ring. Make it official."

"I'm rethinking hiring you, Spencer." Axel frowned. Truth was, he knew he was being dramatic and slightly caveman, but he'd lost the love of his life. He wasn't going to take chances with his best friend.

"I could do it," Libby said quietly, but with a confidence that made Axel believe she absolutely could wipe the floor with him. Still.

"Libby," Archer said. "Do you feel confident taking this case? Though to be honest it's really not about Libby or you, Axel, but our client. How does he feel knowing one of his bodyguards is in danger of her own? Can you safely do your job while watching your back?"

"I'm confident. We're watching our backs anyway. But you're right. It's up to Mr. Coburn." She turned to Axel. "And him alone."

Axel huffed. "He trusts us regardless. For now."

"Then Libby is a trained fighter, and she can do her job. It's why we hired her. If The Eye has targeted her, then don't you think being by her side 24/7 makes even more sense than taking her off the case to be alone in a safe house?"

Libby now shot Archer a dirty look, but kept quiet. He had a point. If Libby worked the protection detail for Coburn, she would be under Axel's watchful eye as well, and he would not let harm come to her. He'd been away from Cheryl. He would be on Libby like glue on a kindergartener's cut-and-paste project.

"For tonight," Archer said, "put him in a motel, watch your backs and the rest of us will interview the victims' families. Someone who lost a loved one is most likely behind the threats and attempts on Harley's life. He's signed the papers refusing safe house care. He strikes me as someone who would find that weak—hiding. And we can't make him."

Thus the forms. If clients kept their regular routines and opted out of the professional advice, then any attempt or injury on them wasn't at the cost of the team. No liability. No suing.

"No, we can't. We'll do as you say." Axel darted

a glance to Libby to confirm, but she stared at the wall. Smoke might as well be streaming from her nostrils.

"Get him to a motel and be sure you're not followed. Also put a tracker in his watch while he sleeps. Better he not know about it." Archer nodded once. "That all?" He frowned and looked to his right. "Not again," he grumbled, and Axel heard a doorbell ring through the computer. Sounded like Archer had company. "Why me?" Archer groused. "Jolie, I'll send an email with orders." He hit the keyboard and the screen went black.

Bridge stood. "Okay, I'll comb through the family files. See if I can discover any of the victims' family members in El Paso around the time of the attempted threats. We can interview them by phone too. I prefer to look folks in the eye when I talk to them, read their body language, but we may not have that kind of time."

Amber stood as well. "I'll contact the detectives working the serial cases in the major Texas cities and get some feedback, gut feelings and I'll also get the case files from the attacks on Harley from the Dallas PD. They may not like talking to bodyguards or PIs too much, but a former homicide detective is another story. They'll be more comfortable with me." She followed Bridge out of the room, Jolie trailing behind with her laptop and iced coffee, leaving him and Libby alone in the conference room.

"That was a low blow, Axel. You made me feel like I wasn't part of the team for the first time. You acted as if I'm incompetent."

He had, but he hadn't meant to. He opened his mouth to apologize as she stood and held up her hand to halt him.

"I don't want to hear excuses. I know why you can be overbearing sometimes. I understand better than anyone. But I never would have made you feel inept or tried to kick you off an assignment."

Shame heated his cheeks. She approached him and her face softened. Libby understood. She'd lost a loved one on the job too. He appreciated her showing him grace.

Then Libby's fist rammed into his diaphragm and his lungs seized, knocking all the air from him. "Consider that a lesson in how to keep your mouth shut." She waltzed from the conference room, leaving him bent at the knees and waiting for his breath to return. Her hit had been quick, sharp and impactful.

Lesson learned.

He had it coming and she was right. But The Eye was the most diabolical killer Axel had ever been up against, and the fact he now had his eyes on Libby terrified him. It should terrify the team.

Libby was formidable but this opponent wasn't to be taken lightly, and she might be outmatched.

They all might be outmatched.

Libby blew down the hall infuriated with Axel, and herself for not finishing the job and putting Axel out cold on the floor. He'd humiliated her and made her feel incompetent among some of the most elite bodyguards she'd ever met. Amber hollered her name, and she turned to the former Memphis homicide detective. Amber had won over fifty shooting championships and was one of the world's top marksmen.

"Hey, Axel's being Axel." Amber tossed her a knowing look.

Libby appreciated Amber's attempt to calm her down, but it was far too late for that. It hadn't been Amber on the other end of his ambush.

"He crossed a line."

"He did," she admitted. "So you know, no one thinks you're incapable of doing your job. I do wish you would have confided about a stalker. How bad has it been? Really?"

She didn't want to admit that it brought up memories from the First Lady's stalker and how that last night had been terrifying. Libby had almost died. Lucas had, but they'd protected the First Lady. Done their jobs. She even checked in on Libby every few months, which was kind and thoughtful. But Libby wanted to pretend that night never happened.

"It's been unnerving." To say the least. "I should have told you. You see why I didn't tell Axel. And before you say it, I know his past. His fears." She knew better than anyone on the team. But Cheryl had taught elementary school kids. She could wield a whistle and a crayon like nobody's business. Libby was a trained agent and a master in martial arts. It was not the same, and she feared Axel saw Cheryl when looking at Libby, and that rankled for more reasons than she wanted to admit or explore.

She was not Cheryl Spears.

What happened to her was tragic, unfair and heinous. And unexpected. Cheryl hadn't fit the serial killer's type. Axel had never dreamed she was in any danger, but this job—Libby—she was always in danger and that was the risk she was willing to take to help others survive brutal attacks and chilling scenarios.

She'd been a protector since her little brother had been pushed down a hill and into a creek when he was thirteen. She had climbed that hill, at only fourteen, and whipped all four boys who'd made it their mission to bully her brother, Tad. All because he wore glasses with thick frames that shrunk his eyes behind them. No one had the right to take away dignity from a human being.

Those boys had run away crying, and Libby had made sure come Monday morning the whole school knew their black eyes and bloody lips had been done by one lone girl.

Tad was never messed with again, but the bullying had taken effect mentally and emotionally. He'd crawled into a cocoon and was never the same person. Even today he kept to himself and worked remotely. But he answered her calls and usually on the first ring. After she'd been attacked protecting the First Lady, Tad had been by her side in the hospital the entire time.

Her heart died that day seeing Lucas die. She knew then she would never fall for a man again and definitely not one she worked alongside. She didn't love Axel romantically, but they were obviously too close in a friendship because he'd lost his mind back there.

She entered the bathroom, splashed cold water on her cheeks then returned to the smaller room where Harley Coburn sipped a cup of coffee and played on his phone. He glanced up. "Ms. Winters. Everything okay?"

He might need to be in the loop about danger, but her emotions weren't any of his business. "Yep. Axel been in here?"

"No. Not yet. You don't look well."

"I'm fine, Mr. Coburn. Thank you for asking. You finish all the paperwork?"

"I did." He smiled. "The admin assistant collected it and brought me this coffee. It's good. Guatemalan?"

"Could be Folgers for all I know. I'm not a coffee connoisseur." Her tone was brusque, and he was paying top dollar for their services. Civility was in order. "I'm sorry. It's been a long day and it's not even past lunchtime."

Harley chuckled. "I imagine all your days are long before it's even lunch. Your bio showed you were a Secret Service agent and protected the First Lady and President. That must have been incredible."

"It was an honor to serve my country." The pat answer and also the truth. "We'll be leaving for a motel, just for the rest of the day and overnight. You can resume your normal activities tomorrow, though you already know we frown upon that."

Harley studied her and then nodded. "You remind me of my older sister. She was a take-charge person. No-nonsense and always looked out for me, fixing up my scraped knees and elbows. You wouldn't know it now, but when I was growing up there wasn't enough money in the world to make me less awkward. In fact, if it hadn't been for the money, I imagine I would have taken a far harder hit from those higher up in the social food chain."

Harley had been bullied. His showy demeanor

and flashy watches and cars now made sense. He was compensating for being a target when he was a kid. "Is she a Secret Service agent now?" Libby asked, and smirked.

Harley sighed. "No. No, she had an accident when we were teenagers and lives in a facility near El Paso. She had a brain injury and never returned to her old self. She's like a small child now. All that spunk and fight that she used to help me—gone."

"I'm sorry to hear that."

He swallowed hard and sniffed. "Thank you."

Axel entered and tossed her a quick glance. "Let's get some lunch, and we'll head to the motel."

"Fine." Libby breezed from the room and strode to the front door. She swept the outdoor perimeter, then Axel and Harley followed.

"What sounds good for lunch, Mr. Coburn?" Axel asked.

"Anything except Italian. I'm not a fan of red sauce. And please call me Harley."

Axel pulled onto the heavily trafficked street and drove half a mile down the road where they ate the best West Texas Tex-Mex while making small talk, but mostly it was a wall of awkward silence between her and Axel. After their meal, they proceeded to the motel, and Axel went inside and checked in.

Axel returned to the SUV and Libby opened the passenger door. "I'll do a sweep while you take him inside." Before he could protest, she exited the vehicle and pulled her weapon. The motel was an L-shape with all outer doors. Nothing extravagant and easy to escape if necessary. No pesky elevators or halls inside. Also, easier to keep watch.

The air was hot and sticky; sweat emerged like an underground fountain around her hairline and nape of her neck, and a distinct eeriness rode on the air. She inhaled the scent of spices from a nearby Mexican restaurant and trash from the overflowing dumpster located behind the motel.

She noted vehicles parked in the area and snapped photos of them and the plate numbers with her cell phone. The rain had finally ceased, but the ominous clouds hovered like Peeping Toms over the Franklin Mountains in all their rocky glory. The wind picked up, blowing old food wrappers and foam cups across the motel's back parking lot. But something else hovered on the wet gale.

They hadn't been followed—she'd made sure of that—and only their team knew of the motel's location.

Didn't mean their vehicles hadn't been LoJack'd. She had a wand and could do a sweep to be sure. Or maybe she was simply on edge. The Eye had ambushed her through the fog, and it appeared he'd stalked her for over a month.

She wasn't safe, and while she had capabilities to care for herself, those skills didn't bring her peace. God gave her peace, but she had a nasty habit of pushing that peace away and exchanging it for worry and anxiety. Even today, after several years, she had PTSD from the blade that had slashed across her throat, nearly taking her life and taking Lucas's. She'd watched in shock and horror as the First Lady's stalker, Renner Ragsdale, had murdered the man Libby loved only hours after they'd talked of marriage.

And if Lucas hadn't been so intent on caring for Libby, he wouldn't have lowered his guard—left the First Lady, who he was supposed to protect at all costs, even over Libby. He would be alive today if he hadn't left the President's wife to save Libby. Her throat had already been slashed and the ambulances called. All he'd had to do was stay inside the panic room, hunkered down with his assigned duty. Renner wouldn't have gotten the jump on him. He had been fleeing when Lucas intercepted him in the doorway.

Libby had been clutching her throat trying to staunch the blood, unable to speak or gasp as she watched Renner murder Lucas before her very eyes.

A quarter of an inch deeper on her own throat,

and her vocal cords would have been severed. She was fully aware God had spared her. Her survival was nothing short of His divine intervention. But Lucas suffered a quick death. She always wondered why God had intervened for her and not Lucas. That was above her pay grade and not her business, but she had been pretty angry for a while. Some days were still hard. Libby couldn't even eat a steak without a mild panic attack at touching the steak knife.

She'd walked away from the Secret Service. Not out of fear or even feelings of ineptness, but because all she could see was Lucas bleeding out, covered in blood, while she tried to keep herself alive. Being on presidential detail became more of a torment than an honor.

Libby rounded the west side of the motel, continuing to snap photos of cars and license plates in order to determine if they were fixtures here or parked for more nefarious reasons.

As she approached the front of the motel again, something bright yellow flapped in the wind. Someone had tucked a paper underneath the windshield of their SUV. Her pulse spiked as she surveyed the area. Same set of cars parked with no new vehicles. The lot was empty of people, but that didn't mean someone wasn't crouching behind a car waiting for her—or Axel.

Libby inched toward the SUV, peeking around

cars and staying on alert. Sweat trickled down her neck and dotted her upper lip, but she kept moving until she approached the Suburban.

A chill traveled down her spine as she dug inside her purse and found a set of tweezers, using them to pluck the paper from the windshield and preserve possible fingerprints while leaving hers out.

Black block letters blared like a tornado siren.

How can you, a woman, defend a killer like him? You're no better than he is. You deserve to die too. You will die too. Maybe tonight. Maybe tomorrow. Watch your back.

Libby's stomach churned as her mind whirled, and she scanned the lot, making sure she was alone. The Eye hadn't left this note. This was about Harley Coburn and the fact she was guarding him. Which meant she had double the trouble. If this was more than an empty threat, Libby could be a target for the same person or people coming after Harley Coburn, and she was already painted with a bull's-eye for The Eye.

Unless… Could The Eye be toying with her on another level to get at Axel? To keep them in chaos and turmoil?

Either way, the threat had hit the mark.

Libby was terrified.

THREE

Shoving the paper in a plastic travel-sized Kleenex package then her blazer pocket, since she had no evidence bag to preserve it, Libby entered the motel room with a quiet calm she did not feel on the inside. No point freaking out Harley after an already eventful morning.

He sat on the sofa in a small living space, scrolling on his phone. Axel stood by the TV perusing a menu. Harley didn't look up, but Axel did and he clearly saw the apprehension pulsing in her eyes. He laid the menu down, glanced at Harley and then returned his focus to Libby as he arched an eyebrow.

He was going to go postal—again. "Can I see you outside?"

Harley finally looked up, phone resting in his palm. "If this involves me, then I'd like to be privy, Ms. Winters."

"It doesn't." Not exactly. Libby pulled a face, and Axel followed her outside. Once the door was closed, she removed the yellow note with the tweezers and held it out. "Here, but hold it with these." Her fingers brushed his as they traded off the threat on sunshiny paper. "I found it on our Suburban after my sweep. About ten minutes time for them to leave it and get out of Dodge."

Axel frowned and read the note, as a line across his brow deepened with each word, becoming a massive divot. "I don't know how anyone would know where we are. We weren't followed. I would have seen."

"Maybe. Maybe not. We're human. We make mistakes."

He grunted his answer. Axel didn't like to make mistakes or admit to them, and Libby wasn't all that keen on admitting it either. "Our business is being staked out or someone else was also on the Coburn estate watching—watching him and saw you. Saw you chase someone into the woods and shoot at them, protecting Coburn."

"What if it's The Eye? Pretending to be a victim's loved one to try and terrify me even more? To toy with us. Throw us off."

"It's possible," Axel replied. "Anything is possible, but it's more likely Harley's little troll. They're furious that a woman is helping protect him when the victims are women. As if you have no compassion or are simply indifferent."

"I'm not."

Axel half smiled. "I know that Libby. You're one of the most compassionate people I know underneath that tough exterior. It's what makes you so good at your job. You care deeply."

Libby's cheeks filled with heat. Axel didn't often give compliments, and it startled her. She expected him to be angrier.

"Which is why what I did earlier made you paralyze my diaphragm." He smirked. "You feel deeply—even the bad feelings like embarrassment and humiliation. That was not my goal."

"I know," she whispered.

Axel shoved his hands in his pockets. "Now that I can breathe again, I can say I shouldn't have done that. I spoke before thinking. It scared me, but that's no excuse for my Neanderthal behavior." He inhaled and let out a slow exhale. "Libby, you mean a lot to me, and I know what this monster is capable of doing—even to you, a force to be reckoned with. It terrifies me to think he's watching us and has been watching you. And it disappoints me that you didn't trust me enough to tell me a month ago."

Axel admitting he was wrong had been difficult for him, and she cared a lot about him as well. She laid a gentle hand on his forearm. "I should have. You're right. But what you said this morning is exactly why I didn't tell you. I don't need you camping out on my couch or guarding my front door every night."

"I wouldn't have—"

"Yes, you would," she said through a smile.

He returned it. "I would."

She sighed. He didn't need further reprimanding, but they might both need their friendship terms restated. "We're friends, and friends trust each other. They don't go off the rails without thinking. Lovers do that, and we are not married. That's why we work, Axel. Remember? So have your feelings changed or are you just wound too tight? Do we need to draw a new line and keep it professional, or can you treat me as an equal while still being my best friend?"

Axel's Adam's apple bobbed as he swallowed hard. "I can color within the lines, Libs. Harley, this case… I'm wound too tight. But that doesn't mean I won't worry about you or watch your back, and I can't promise I won't treat you like someone I want to stay alive. But I recognize you are an equal. You can kick serious butt."

"Including yours." She smirked. "Say it," she prompted.

Axel chuckled. "All you're missing is holding me down with spit dangling off your lips as a threat."

Gross. Boys. "You scared of spit, Axel?"

"No."

"Scared to admit I can take you down?"

"No. Because you can't. You got me in the diaphragm, and I'll give you that. But I'm stronger than you physically, and that's a fact." He was literally daring her to try this moment, and she was relieved that the subject had lightened in tone. And she was even happier that the lines were still drawn and his feelings hadn't changed.

But that didn't explain the teeniest pang in her chest when he made it clear that nothing had indeed changed. She got what she wanted.

"If we weren't on duty with a potential threat nearby, I'd so sweep your leg like Johnny in *Karate Kid* and watch you cry."

"Hurting me would give you joy then?"

She snorted. "Immeasurable, Axel. Immeasurable. But I'd have to help you up and you weigh more than a grizzly, and I'd prefer not to throw out my back."

"Wow, you're killing me with all this flattery."

Speaking of being generous, she decided to keep up the fun banter. She needed it as things were turning heavy emotionally. "You didn't actually say you're sorry, just you shouldn't have done it. I want my actual apology." Libby folded her arms over her chest and tapped her foot.

His eyes darkened and he leaned in. "How do you want it?" He held out his hand. "Handshake?" He lifted it up. "High five?" He leaned in farther and that right eyebrow of his inched upward. "Kiss?"

A kiss from Axel? Her insides flushed. She'd be lying if she said it had never crossed her mind. He was attractive, kind, noble, a man of faith and fun to be around. But they worked together and her heart was locked up tight; she'd made sure of it. The few times it had crossed her mind, she took the thought captive and shoved it into the vault.

"Your word. I want to hear the words." Axel was a man of his word and if he said it, she could count on it, rely on it. Trust in it. Even though she already knew he was sorry.

His face softened and he took her hands in his, her stomach fluttering. "I am so sorry for making you feel less than. I am sorry for humiliating you in front of our friends and colleagues. I trust you implicitly. Please forgive me."

Tears burned the backs of her eyes, which was unexpected. The intensity and sincerity in Axel's eyes moved her deeply, and she almost forgot that his touch had sent a schoolgirl flutter in her belly. "I forgive you," she choked out. "And thank you."

"Good. Let's go babysit."

She laughed at that. A lot of their job felt like babysitting.

Inside, Harley watched the news and ate a bag of popcorn they'd brought with them. Axel took the first sweep, and they'd trade off each hour until after 8:00 p.m. when they'd take shifts so the other could get a few hours of sleep.

She made small talk with Harley and read on her phone. She hid that she still loved clean romance novels and would never cough up that secret. Clients didn't need to know she was a romantic at heart—or had been. Now she lived vicariously through fictional characters.

Hours passed and the sun finally dipped behind the Franklin Mountains and then the horizon. Archer had sent over victims' files, and they'd helped Bridge and Amber research family members and past boyfriends, working up logical profiles of who might actually be after Harley. They all had a motive, and most of them probably daydreamed at least once about killing the brute who had snuffed out their loved ones' lives. But not everyone who threatened murder or wished for it carried it out. The right circumstances and personality had to come into play. That's why they needed to do background checks.

Three of the victims had family members who had done prison time for assault and battery. One had been through anger management classes due to road rage. These were likely their suspects since they already had a bent toward criminality.

Axel ran out to grab food and returned with white paper sacks filled with burgers, fries and onion rings. In the other hand he carried a drink holder with four drinks.

Smiling, Axel handed her two of the cups. "Peace offering. Peanut butter milkshake to go with your Diet Dr Pepper with a real shot of cherry."

Her favorites. "Thank you."

"I might have eaten the cherry."

"Per usual. I am not surprised." She laughed and sipped her drink.

"Y'all like an item or something?" Harley asked, and unwrapped his grilled chicken sandwich.

"No," they said in unison. Too fast. Too adamant.

Harley's eyebrows raised. "I see."

She feared he wasn't seeing anything or maybe she and Axel were the blind ones. "Harley, have you had any contact with the victims' families since their deaths? Anyone approach you? We'd like to hear it from you, not reports." She wanted to see if his story would change.

Harley chewed through a grin. "Subject change like whiplash. Nice." After a swig of his sweet tea, he wiped his mouth. "After it leaked on social media six months ago that I'd been brought in for questioning, Paul DeVries showed up outside my work with a ball bat, and I watched as he smashed the headlights out of my Porsche. Not a fan. He said I was going to rot in hot places and Security showed up and escorted him off the lot then proceeded to call the cops, who said they were surprised he hadn't taken the bat to me and one of them muttered, 'Pity.'"

Libby wasn't shocked the police had been lax. They believed he was the killer, though "hoped" might be a better word. She imagined their response time had been slower too. Didn't happen all the time, but sometimes.

"The letters with death threats have been nonstop, the latest only three days ago. I have turned them all in, but apparently no prints and no way to know who sent them. After two more incidents within the past three weeks, with Paul and then with Josh Ramos and Vinny Wallace, I stopped calling the cops altogether and hired y'all. I hope you'll be unbiased too. I didn't kill those women. None of them."

Harley had maintained his innocence in all the questionings and kept to the same answers. Not verbatim as if they were rehearsed, but overall the same accounts every time and just now with them. Vinny Wallace had found him outside a gas station and sucker punched him. When Harley was down, he'd gone to town on his face and torso, leaving two ribs broken and one floating, his eyes both blackened, lip split and a concussion. Vinny had also been arrested on three separate occasions for drunk and disorderly behavior and battery.

Libby checked her Apple watch. Almost 9:00 p.m. "My turn." She stood and stretched then holstered her gun.

"I can go." Axel stood too.

"I'm not tired. I just needed to stretch."

"I know, but I'm good to go and can take it until morning."

Axel held eye contact, and Libby's insides raged with fire. She was not stupid. He was trying to keep her from going on her watch after dark. After he'd sincerely apologized. It was like her giving her anxiety to God and feeling peace, then yanking it back. God had more patience than Libby.

"I'll be fine." She blew past him, shot him a dirty look and closed the door, hearing Axel lock it with more force than necessary. He was angry too. Well boo-hoo.

Drawing her weapon in one hand and small flashlight in the other, she began the walk around the L-shaped motel. Traffic and night birds echoed in the distance. A door slamming closed put her on pause, but then she heard children laughing. A family.

Most of the same cars were in place, but as she moved to the back of the motel, the creepy sensations from earlier rose in goose bumps along her arms and her scalp prickled.

"Libby!"

Axel? "What are you doing out here? You should be with Harley."

"He's locked in tight and fine. I'm worried about you and don't start. I already told you I'd be worried."

Libby fumed. This was why she didn't want to be romantically involved with a coworker. He'd left their client to protect her. The opposite of what they were supposed to be doing, and they weren't even romantically involved! "You've shirked your duty and you own this company. I'm not your client. Go back—"

Gunfire cracked through the air and Axel grunted.

He'd been hit.

Axel winced at the burning pain in his upper left arm and crouched in the dark as another shot fired. This wasn't The Eye's style. He liked it up close and personal, and shooting Axel would be too easy for the twisted monster. Whoever left the threatening note earlier must be behind this.

Libby was right. He shirked his duty to Harley because he was concerned about her. He never should have left him, but if he hadn't been out here with Libby, she could be dead right now.

"Come on," Libby said, and grabbed his arm,

sending a flinch through him. "I'll read you the riot act later. How bad are you hit?"

That would be worse than the bullet. "I don't know. I can't see anything! The wound's on fire."

Another shot sounded, and a bullet hit the brick above them. "On three, head for the dumpster. Three!" she hollered, omitting any other numbers.

They rushed to the dumpster, which reeked, and crouched behind it. "You think it's just the one?" he asked.

"I don't know. Could be two. One to distract or kill us, and the other one could be in the motel room right now where you should be protecting our client."

He had no words. She was right.

"Here's what we're going to do. I'm going to take off running and head for Harley. You get the SUV started and ready to peel out. My place is ten minutes from here, and it's the best and only real choice we have."

Axel didn't have time to argue. Libby was cool, calm and collected. Large and in charge and he'd always admired that about her. Couldn't say the same about him right now.

"Axel, can you do that? Are you hospital hit or bathroom medicine cabinet okay?" Her voice held easy concern.

"I can do it."

"Give me thirty seconds before you bolt. Make sure I have the shooter off of you and onto me."

Axel squeezed her hand. "Be careful."

"Thirty seconds." Libby sprinted into the dark, and the unseen shooter fired another round. Axel prayed Libby would make it in time. Thirty seconds felt like thirty days. But he counted them down and bolted for the Suburban. He'd parked a few spaces down from their room since all the spots in front of their room had been occupied when they'd arrived.

He backed out and left his lights off then slowly crept up to the cars directly in front of the motel. He didn't dare flash his lights to signal he was ready.

Ten seconds passed then twenty.

Had Libby been intercepted? Taken? Killed? His heart hammered against his ribs.

Finally, the door opened and Libby exited first then Harley emerged wearing a Kevlar vest and helmet. They sprinted to the car, and Libby threw open the back passenger door, thrusting Harley inside before shutting it and jumping in the front seat.

As they pulled from the parking lot, another shot was fired and hit the SUV, but they'd had it bulletproofed.

"How were we found?" Harley demanded, and threw the helmet from his head.

Libby winced. They hadn't wanded the car because they were tangling with each other. He was going to hear about it from her. And himself, and Archer. They'd endangered all their lives because Libby was right—they weren't on their A game. They were battling each other and missing steps with their paying client. What would this mean for them? What did it mean in general?

If she pulled back on their friendship, he'd lose his confidant. Libby was his sounding board; they could throw verbal punches and banter without missing a beat. He loved her wit and sarcasm. She was the first person he called on a bad day—or a good one. And they attended church together. They had deep discussions on faith and theology. Who would he do all that with?

"We can find out soon enough," Libby replied, and turned on the overhead light. "You're pretty bloody, Axel. Stop at the gas station up ahead and let me inspect you for myself."

"No can do, Libs. We don't know how far behind us the shooter might be or how many there are."

"You haven't been on your phone or told anyone your location? Not even work?" Libby asked Harley.

"No. I promise. I'm not stupid."

The only other choice was they'd been bugged, and it could have been at any point except in the parking lot at their office. They had a serious security system installed, which included state-of-the-art cameras. Archer monitored it 24/7. He would have seen it.

Maybe Axel wasn't the only one going off the rails. Maybe their friendship had grown closer than they'd realized. The thought sent an ache through his bones. He would have never let it slide if it had been Archer. He'd never have left that motel room to check on him either. He knew sticking with the client was the right thing, but his heart had run the show, and that scared him.

"Go past my place, and we'll sweep the car and his person then return to my house. Not ideal I know, but it's our best option for now." She called Archer and gave him the details. Based on her physical movements and carefully worded answers, Archer knew that they'd dropped the ball. He'd hear about it later.

About two miles past Libby's subdivision, he pulled to the side of the road and Libby snagged the wand. "Harley, out of the car so I can detect if you have any bugs or trackers on you."

Harley hopped out and removed his vest. Libby wanded him. "He's clean."

After he climbed back inside the vehicle, Libby crept around the Suburban with the wand, running it high and low, circling around.

"Why did you end up shot? If they're after me."

"I'm the middleman."

"You should be wearing the vest then. Not me." Harley snorted. "You know I understand these people are hurting. They've lost someone they love. But targeting a man who hasn't been found guilty seems reckless, don't you think?"

"Grief can make a man do things he never thought he would do. It shuts down the logical part of the brain, becomes irrational. I'm not condoning the behavior, but I understand it." Axel flipped on the light again and unbuttoned his shirt, inspecting his wound. It was a through and through that needed stitches, but he could have Libby do it. She was trained, and he didn't want to sit in a hospital half the night for two or three stitches.

The wand whirred and buzzed as Libby stood near the driver's-side front tire. "We got us a bogie," she called, and Axel stepped outside the car, kneeling beside her.

"You see it?" he asked.

"Not yet. It's a little bugger. Literally," she quipped, frowning. "I dropped the ball. I could make excuses that you made me mad and we had a row, but the truth is I didn't do my job. I'm sorry."

"Hey, I didn't do mine either. We have to do better."

"That's what Archer said. He's ticked."

"Understandable." Before she could bring up the whole crossing lines thing again, he changed the subject. "I need three stitches. You up for that?"

"Yeah. Nothing will make me happier than piercing you with a needle. I know why you were outside with me. And it landed with a bullet to your arm. Notice, not mine. I'm in one piece. So who actually needs babysitting?" She laid on her back and reached up, feeling around the rim. "I actually believed you when you said you were sorry."

"I am. I also said I can't promise I won't be concerned about you, and I had good reason. You were being shot at. That could have been you, and I'm not as good with a needle and thread as you."

"Is that a sexist remark? That women sew."

"No, it's a fact your hand is far steadier than mine and last I remember, you do crochet."

"I tried crocheting. Stab it. Strangle it. Pull out its guts. Throw it off the cliff. The method appealed."

"What, are you on serial killer DIY sites now?"

"Ha. Ha." Libby stood up with a small, but sophisticated GPS tracker between her fingers. "My guess is The Eye placed this here at the estate, and that's why he was so quick to grab me. I'd interrupted him." She smashed it with the heel of her boot then picked it up and pocketed it to show Archer. He might know where it had been purchased and that would give them a lead on the culprit.

"I agree with you. Are you sure we should take Harley to your house?"

"We have the tracker. It's disabled and it's the only one. I don't love clients knowing where I live, but I seriously doubt I have anything a rich man like Coburn would want."

"Fair enough."

They reentered the SUV.

"Well? Are we safe now?" Harley asked.

Axel wasn't one to pull any punches. "No. None of us are safe."

FOUR

Libby drove into her garage, her stomach in a tangle of knots for dozens of reasons. She had dropped the ball with wanding the car, and Archer had—in his quiet way—reprimanded her over it. She could take the chewing out; she deserved it. She and Axel had been more about each other than their client and should be fired. But from here on out, she was going to focus solely on Harley, and so help her, she'd make Axel too.

Axel.

If he hadn't been outside the motel, he wouldn't have been shot. A world without Axel felt so wrong. Tragic. She leaned on him heavily and hadn't even realized it until he'd been hit with that bullet. That was dangerous territory.

Now she was bringing a client to her home, and she didn't love the idea. But they were close, and she had no other choice. Not really. "Home sweet home," she muttered. Her home was a modest one, cozy and homey. To Harley Coburn it would be a cracker box or something one would see on a tiny homes show. Not that she cared, but it was simply weird having him here.

"Are you going to be okay, Mr. Spears? Should we have gone to a hospital?" Harley asked, his hand on the door handle.

"I'll be fine. Don't worry." Axel unfolded from the vehicle and Harley followed suit. The garage door opened into the kitchen full of stainless-steel appliances and white shaker cabinets with butcher block countertops. Libby had followed the farmhouse trend. But she loved it and didn't feel like such a sheep.

"Did you bake cookies?" Axel asked.

She tossed him a withering glance. Really? "You know I don't bake."

"I smell cookies."

"It's my wax melt scents." She dropped her purse on the kitchen counter. "We need to stitch you up."

"You're going to stitch him?" Harley asked, his voice and cheeks wan.

"Why don't you make yourself at home. I'll show you to your room for the night, and you can settle in while I take care of Axel." She looked at her partner. "My bathroom. Now."

"Yes, ma'am," Axel said, and saluted her then headed into her bedroom off the kitchen where her bathroom was located.

"He knows his way around. You sure nothing is going on between you two?" Harley asked as he rolled his suitcase across the wooden-looking tile floors of the kitchen, through her open house plan and upstairs.

"We're colleagues and friends—and he's my boss too." And it was none of his business. Harley wasn't asking because he wanted to pursue her, was he? The answer was nope. Not that he wasn't attractive. He definitely was, but the cockiness that shrouded him was a turnoff. Although, Axel carried himself in a similar manner but she knew it was pure confidence. Axel was the most capable man she knew and she admired that about him, but after Cheryl's death that confidence took a hit. She quickly saw the difference from the time she'd worked with him when he was FBI and after the tragedy. Still, he carried himself as if his world hadn't been dented.

She led Harley down the hall to the last room on the right, which had its own private bath. "I hope it's acceptable. I have plenty of toiletries in the bathroom, and the streaming services are logged in so you can watch whatever you like."

He surveyed the room done in several shades of tranquil blue and abstract art. "It's nice. It's... well... I just didn't see you as soft. Your house is quite feminine."

She arched an eyebrow. Yes, she was hardcore

and serious about her job. She was a fighter and strong and could use a gun better than Annie Oakley, but that didn't mean she was hardened. Libby had a feminine side, enjoyed makeup and wearing pretty dresses and heels. When the situation called for it. "Can't judge a book by its cover."

"No. No, you can't. I appreciate your hospitality, and I didn't mean that contrast as an insult just a pleasant surprise." His smile was sheepish, and he shrugged and turned on a lamp by the bed.

The man could be charming. She'd give him that. Maybe his cockiness was overcompensation for insecurity. He'd mentioned he'd been bullied as a kid. Those kinds of things could stick with a person for decades—even for people with McDuck money. "Thanks." Libby might have been judging the book by the cover herself. "If you need anything let me know."

"Will do. Thanks again."

She nodded and closed the door behind her. Now to deal with Axel and his stitches. She hurried down the stairs and paused at the open bathroom door, hearing a clinking noise. She peeked into the bath. Axel sat on her white plush vanity stool holding a bottle of her perfume, which she never wore to work. Amber had allergies, plus wearing perfume, while perfectly fine, could make her appear less tough. Which was why she kept to muted colors, simple ponytails and a little mascara and bronzer so she didn't look like she had the flu.

He had the cap in his hand and lifted the bottle to his nose and inhaled. A soft hum left his lips and her belly dipped. Axel clearly liked her perfume but she'd never worn it around him, even when hanging out. Those times usually came off long shifts of working and having meals or riding horses at his ranch. Nothing that required fragrance.

After capping it, he placed it where he found it and rifled through her makeup brushes as if he'd been given a foreign object and was told to figure it out.

"Hey," she said, and entered. He held up the makeup brush.

"I didn't realize you wore makeup."

"I have a life outside work and hanging out with you. What is it with men tonight?" she muttered.

"What do you mean?" he asked, and put the brush back in the holder and began unbuttoning his shirt.

"Harley said my house was feminine and so opposite of me. Whatever. I am a woman." She opened a door under her sink and pulled out a first aid kit.

"I know you're a woman," he said, and she

paused. Had his voice lowered into a huskiness she rarely heard or was she imagining things? "For the record."

Maybe her weird feelings tonight had nothing to do with Axel and everything to do with a stalker who might be The Eye or that two separate men were targeting her. The scar across her neck throbbed. Phantom pain every time she thought about that night.

She laid the kit on the counter and opened it. "Three you say?"

"Stitches?"

"No," she drawled with sarcasm. "Strikes, and you're out. Yes, stitches."

He chuckled. "I think so."

She brought out the antiseptic and doused a sterile gauze patch. "Gonna sting, bro."

"Bring it, *bro*," he stressed, and gave her a quizzical expression.

Not her usual term, but she needed to remind herself and maybe him that they were buds. Bros in a sense. Friends. In fact, Axel should flat-out forget she was a woman who could on occasion smell nice.

And she needed to forget he was a man. A very masculine one. His skin wasn't pale like hers, but perpetually tan, probably from some of his Native American heritage. Sharp straight nose and chiseled jawline with high cheekbones declared it if his shiny black mane and eyes didn't.

He shot her another quizzical look, and she cleared her throat and focused on his wound not his face. "You're bad at math. Try six." She laid the gauze on his skin and he winced. "Baby."

He smirked, revealing a small dimple on his right cheek.

"You want lidocaine?"

"I'm a big baby. What do you think?"

She pulled out a syringe and injected the lidocaine. His jaw twitched, and she tucked away a smile at his attempt to be a tough guy after her verbal gouge. "Just need to give it a minute or two."

The room grew quiet, building an odd wall of tension between them. She spotted a faint scar on his shoulder blade and touched it before thinking better. "Where'd you get that?"

Axel glanced at her finger on his arm and then up at her, holding her gaze for a beat longer than made her comfortable. "Rock climbing. Faulty equipment and I fell on a tree root. Sliced it open. Twelve stitches. So I can take six."

"Scars. Always there to remind us of pain." She used foundation to try and help cover her own scar running across her throat. Never would be able to let that part of her past go. The scar wouldn't let her.

Axel looked at her through the mirror. His eyes revealed empathy, saying it all; he understood pain, loss. Grief and helplessness. "I smelled your perfume."

She laughed at his abrupt statement. "Yeah?"

"You wear that on dates I don't know about?"

"Are you supposed to know about my dates?" She threaded the catgut through the sterile needle.

"Am I not supposed to?" he countered.

"Hold still, big baby." Dates? Axel knew she didn't go on them at all anymore. They shared the same aversion. What was he actually trying to discover? She pressed the needle into his flesh. "You feel that?"

"Not really."

"Then let's Frankenstein ya." She slipped the needle through his flesh, weaving in and out, acutely aware that he was studying her, and it unsettled her. "Last one." After finishing and cutting the thread, she tossed the needle and admired her work. "You did so good you deserve a sucker."

Axel stood. Slipped on his shirt and buttoned it. "Thanks, Doc." He tugged her ponytail. "I like it."

"The stitches?"

"The perfume," he murmured.

Libby's insides puddled. What on earth was

wrong with her? With him? "Oh," she responded. "I wear it for special occasions."

His eyebrows inched north as if he was filing away her response. "Harley in his room?"

"Yeah. You tired?"

"Not really. You want me to take the other room upstairs or the one by the front door?" he asked, and walked into her bedroom. It had never been awkward before. He'd hung the painting above her bed over a year ago. Cleaned the carpet when she'd moved in and helped her put her bedframe together. No big deal. But now for some reason, she was very aware of his presence in here. A very masculine presence with the hint of aftershave she feared would linger when he left.

He paused at the chest of drawers and glanced at the framed photo positioned in the center.

Libby and Lucas.

The night he'd proposed and she'd said yes. But she'd had no idea it was coming. She and Lucas were private people and didn't need wild over-the-top proposal videos to share. She'd finished a 10K and he'd been at the finish line with a banner that read: *Finish our race together?*

They were in shorts, and she had been sweaty but happy.

Axel met her eyes and held her gaze for one beat…two…three until she inwardly squirmed. She couldn't tell what he was thinking but it unnerved her. "You—" her voice cracked. "—you want to watch our usual?"

"Parks and Rec?"

"Well of course." Nothing like early 2000s sitcoms.

"Popcorn?"

"You make it," she said, "and I'll get the episode queued up after I do a quick perimeter sweep to be safe."

After their earlier heated discussions, he kept silent now. Good. She could do a sweep as easy as he could. Once she returned from a nice and quiet search, she found the sitcom on her most watched streaming service as the aroma of popping popcorn filled the living space with scents of butter and all around deliciousness.

The microwave dinged and Axel said, "Go ahead and start it. You want a Coke or fizzy water?"

"Fizzy."

The cabinet door opened and closed, and then he carried two drinks and a bowl full of fake buttery goodness to the couch, plopping down beside her. Close. Too close. Not that he was doing anything different. They shared an ottoman for their feet many times, which meant sitting close, but tonight it felt different.

Axel handed her the fizzy drink, and she tucked it into the drink holder in the console of the couch. The theme song ended and the show started, but Libby couldn't concentrate with Axel's leg resting against hers, or the knowledge that someone—or possibly two different people—wanted her dead.

Libby was off tonight. From the moment they entered her house, Axel could tell she'd been on edge, tiptoeing around him. Granted, she did have a man in her home who'd been questioned in the murders of several women, and there had been more than one attempt on her life, but this was altogether different.

They had watched three episodes of *Parks and Recreation*, and Libby had fidgeted the entire time, even curling her feet up on the couch instead of sharing the ottoman as if she wanted to escape him. She said she'd forgiven him and wasn't mad, but she was not herself this evening and it didn't have anything to do with nearly dying. It had to do with the two of them.

Something seemed to have shifted in the bathroom earlier. But he didn't want to think about that right now.

"You think whoever installed the tracker left a print?" Libby asked, and he was thankful for the distraction.

The tracker placed on the Suburban had been sophisticated but not government grade. They might be able to trace it from the manufacturer to wherever it was sold and from there find the purchaser's name. "I hope so, but whoever placed it there was quick and calculated, knowing he wouldn't be identified on cameras, and he must have had the equipment with him already because he didn't know we were going to meet with Harley today. He's done this before. Professional."

Libby heaved a sigh. "I don't like that."

"I don't either." He put his hand in the bowl of popcorn at the same time as Libby, and their fingers met. She jerked back like she'd been burned. "Wow, you're jumpy tonight."

Her cheeks reddened and she looked away. So. Not. Like. Her. "I have reason don't you think?" she snapped.

What was going on with her? Was it the stalker weighing on her mind or was it something else? He could handle it if it was the stalker. If it was far more personal, he wouldn't be able to handle that. He liked them the way they were. But...but something was happening that he didn't want to deal with. He'd rather pretend her issues were about a killer.

"Libby, it's okay to be fearful. The Eye has been watching and invaded your home. I admit, I feel guilty about that. He's likely targeting you to get to me." He shifted on the couch and took her hand. She stiffened but he didn't let go. "We're going to make sure we keep each other safe and stay smart from here on out. No more blunders."

Axel wasn't Lucas Reed. He would not make the same mistakes. Mostly because unlike Lucas, Axel wasn't madly in love with Libby Winters. And also, he had to quit projecting his failures with Cheryl onto Libby. If he could do that, he wouldn't slip up anymore.

"It's not that."

"Then what is it?" Axel asked.

"Nothing. It's probably that."

For the first time ever, Libby was acting like a woman. Talking around mountains and keeping him clueless. Where was the woman who spoke her feelings, whether he wanted her to or not, with clarity and bluntness? He wasn't into riddles.

Axel's phone rang, and he wasn't sure if he was grateful or irritated. "It's Archer," he told Libby, and she nodded and turned down the TV volume. "We found a tracker. It's been smashed." Axel updated him and noted he'd send the tracker to the private lab they used in the morning. "I took a photo, though. Sending it now." Axel uploaded and texted the photo.

"This is pricey," Archer said. "But it can be purchased from a reputable online company. I'll look into it. Get back to you when I have something. Bridge and Amber have a few leads. We can discuss later. How's our client? He change his mind about who guards him?"

"Not so far. He's in his room. I'll check on him in about thirty minutes and do a sweep of the house."

"Good. Keep me posted, and if you need reinforcements, call Amber or Bridge. They know to be on standby." Archer yawned. "I'm exhausted."

"I wonder why."

"I really don't want to have this conversation again, Axel. I'm doing the right thing. I'm keeping everyone safe. That's all I know to do." Axel heard a knock and Archer groan. "Unbelievable. It's still illegal to murder a person, right?"

"Last I checked."

"Even if it *feels* like self-defense?" He chuckled. "I gotta go or that banging is going to cause issues and I might snap." He ended the call, and Axel shook his head. Archer couldn't keep going like this forever.

"Last you checked, what?" Libby asked.

"Nothing. Just Archer being Archer. He's going to look into the GPS tracker put on the car. See where it might have been sold from. You wanna just let the TV roll or are you going to bed?" Bed, where the first thing Libby would see before sleeping was Lucas's photo and he would be the first thing she'd see in the morning too.

He'd kept photos of Cheryl around his place

too at first, but now it was down to only their wedding photo on the mantel. He'd never not love Cheryl, but the photos were too hard for him to look at daily and stunted his growth forward. Everyone grieved differently, and while having a photo in the bedroom might comfort Libs, it had done the opposite for Axel.

Axel knew he'd see Cheryl again someday and the grief had ebbed. Was Libby still grieving Lucas? Is that why she had him so close still? And why did seeing his photo cause an itch like poison ivy in his chest? It shouldn't. She had loved Lucas like he'd loved Cheryl. Being slightly jealous of a man who had passed seemed childish and insensitive, but he felt what he felt. He just didn't know why.

"We have a big day tomorrow. You take the next sweep outside. I'm going to bed. Take the upstairs room. I'll keep downstairs covered," Libby said.

He agreed and carried the empty popcorn bowl minus a handful of unpopped kernels to the kitchen, dumped it out and placed it in the dishwasher. Libby rinsed her glass and his and added them in. Her arm brushed his, sending a little wave of chill bumps, and the perfume he'd inhaled earlier sprang to mind. Sweet. A little spicy. Intoxicating.

Wow, he was tired. Libby's perfume shouldn't be doing a number on him.

"Good night, Axel," Libby whispered.

A mountain had grown in his throat, and he swallowed down the aching lump. "Night, Libs."

She padded to her room and closed the door with a quiet click. Axel blew a heavy breath and turned off the kitchen light then did a perimeter check before he grabbed his bags from the car and toted them upstairs. He paused at Harley's door and listened. A popular crime show played. Axel had enough real crime to last a lifetime. He slipped across the hall and changed into gym shorts and a T-shirt then glanced into Libby's backyard. The moon cast eerie shadows along the lawn.

Then one of them moved.

FIVE

Axel gripped his gun and raced from the bedroom downstairs where Libby stood at the back door with her own weapon drawn.

"You saw him?" he whispered.

"Heard him outside my window. I'm going to go out the living room window on the other side and take the back."

"I'm going out the front." Axel headed for the front door and slipped outside into the muggy thick air. Keeping in the shadows, Axel moved in the direction he'd seen the figure.

This could be his chance to take down The Eye.

He crept along the side of the house but the figure was gone, no longer lurking in the shadows. Axel met Libby in the backyard. She shook her head. "He's gone now."

"The guy must have heard us and bolted. I'm going to drive around the neighborhood, see if I can find him. You stick with Harley."

Was The Eye playing mind games with them again by showing up in the shadows? He'd played mind games with Axel for years while Axel had hunted him across Texas, toying with him to show he was superior.

And maybe he was.

Maybe he had been.

He jogged to the vehicle and cranked the engine, then backed out and drove around the neighborhood, but it was quiet and dark. No sign of him.

Finally, he gave up, feeling totally defeated, and returned to Libby's house. She sat at the table, her fingers tented. "Harley never woke, or he kept to his room. Probably better he doesn't know."

"Probably so."

"Although we assume it was The Eye, it could have been a victim's family member out there and they're the party who put the tracker on the car."

He leaned against the counter. "We damaged it before we arrived. The Eye has been here before. He may not realize Harley is present. I think it was him, but we can't rule anything out. Harley is paying us to protect him. Did you actually lay eyes on him?"

"No."

They both bolted up the stairs, and Axel lightly knocked on Harley's door. No answer. He cracked it and Harley lay in bed on his side, his face bathed in moonlight. Dead asleep. Relief relaxed Axel's shoulders and he closed the door and made a thumbs-up motion for Libby.

"Could have done without that scare," she whispered on the stairs.

"Preach."

"I'm going to try going back to bed once again."

Axel smiled. "I'll be up a while. I'll wake you at three. Harley signed waivers so we'll be escorting him to work tomorrow. Fun. Fun."

"That will tire me right out just thinking about it." She grinned. "Good night again," she said, and disappeared into her bedroom. Hopefully, tomorrow would be an easier day. But his gut clenched, warning him nefarious things were just beginning.

Would he be enough to protect Libby?

Libby yawned and sipped her Americano with honey and heavy cream. They'd run through a local coffee shop on the way to CoburnPharma in downtown El Paso, though they had two other facilities in Dallas and Austin. After the lurker last night, she and Axel hadn't slept soundly. It was evident in his stubble he'd omitted shaving this morning due to being too tired and lazy.

Harley on the other hand appeared fresh as a daisy, unaware of their visitor. Due to the fact it could have been a victim's family member hunting him, they informed him. He wasn't thrilled, but he hadn't called them off of protecting him yet either.

CoburnPharma was a brick twenty story building used for research and business. They had other manufacturing locations. Harley worked on the nineteenth floor. Not quite the penthouse, where his parents and uncle kept offices and large conference rooms.

"We'll escort you to your office. One of us will be outside the door while the other stays in the background," Libby said as they entered the lobby and strode toward the elevator. She held up a small device that looked like a man's dress shirt button. "This is for an emergency. It goes over your collar button, and you can press it if you get into a pinch and need us ASAP." She pointed to his shirt. "May I?" she asked as they entered the elevator.

He nodded and she stepped into his personal space, which gave her a hint of pricey masculine cologne. He already dressed to the nines, and the scent added to how rich the man was. She fitted it over the button like a glove. Archer had access to spy gadgets. Pens. Glasses that were cameras and recorders. She never asked questions. Libby simply loved them.

"A single push alerts us on our Apple watches through an app. Press it."

Harley pressed the fake shirt button, and Axel's and Libby's phones beeped like an Amber Alert as a streak of red flashed across the screen of their watches: 911...911...911 on a repeating loop. She showed him then went into her app and disarmed it. Axel's stopped flashing and beeping too.

"Y'all are like James Bond."

He wasn't wrong. Libby grinned. "Bond is better looking and more sophisticated than Axel."

Axel raised an eyebrow.

Libby chuckled and Harley laughed with her. Axel's amusement lit up his ebony eyes. "Any questions for us?" she asked Harley as they exited the elevator and walked to Harley's office, securing it as safe.

"I'm going to feel weird if you stand guard over my office. I get whispers enough as is and they know personal security is here, but still. Is that completely necessary?"

Axel pinched his lips together. "Once we clear the building and note that all employees are legit, I can make myself scarce but be close. Do not stand or be in front of your windows. If we need to rearrange your desk, we can. However, you can't leave your office, not even to use the bathroom—"

"I have a bathroom in my office and my desk has already been moved since the first time I was fired on—outside my house."

"Smart and noted. You can't leave your office without notifying me by text. I don't have to escort you, but I do want to clear the area before you enter. Can you do that?"

Harley nodded. "I don't think any of my employees are serving me death threats. They have too much to risk—like their job. And we pay well here."

Libby held in the eye roll. His privilege and pride dripped like sour honey—if that was a thing.

"Still, protocol." Axel gave him a stern look.

"I usually go to lunch around one. Do I need to order in?"

"Not unless you want to," Axel said. "Sorry, but we'll be on you like you're a celebrity if you leave the building."

"Or the President," Harley quipped, and looked at Libby.

"Or the President," she murmured. Her memories were bittersweet concerning her time with the Secret Service. "Now that we have you secure in your office, we'll do a sweep of the building and do it periodically. While we do that, you are to stay locked inside."

Chill bumps broke out along Libby's arms. She

glanced around, searching for anyone lasered in on her, but nothing appeared out of the ordinary. Axel touched her elbow and spoke through his eyes, asking what was wrong.

She shook her head. "You see anything out of the ordinary, let us know."

"I'll do my best," Harley said.

After leaving his office, Axel and Libby split the floors. Axel took the bottom half and Libby the upper half to the twentieth story. She walked the long sterile hall of Harley's floor with offices flanking it, and then into a large area full of cubicles. People slurped coffee, gossiped among themselves and talked on their phones. Nothing suspicious.

Once she cleared the space, she took the elevator up one floor to the top, then she'd hit the floors below and meet back in Harley's office with him and Axel.

A set of icy fingers walked along her back, her gut warning her danger prowled. She tried to never ignore her gut. Better safe than dead.

She gripped her gun as the elevator opened to the twentieth story. Only three offices were occupied up here, but they were empty today as his parents and uncle were out of town and working remotely. There were several large conference rooms and storage areas for lab and research equipment according to the blueprints they'd been given earlier.

As she exited the elevator, Libby's unease continued, which might be more about impending doom from The Eye than someone hiding in wait to make another attempt on Harley's life. The Eye was a formidable opponent, and he had yet to lose.

Of course, she trusted God with her life. But that didn't mean that she was safe in body. Her soul, yes. Body…? The Eye had even bested Axel, and he was a skilled and trained agent with great gut instinct and intuition.

Libby walked the empty hall. The floor was secure and quiet. Her nerves were jumpy as she suspected. She punched the elevator button and blew a sigh of relief. As the door opened, a black-clad figure charged her from the side, startling her and toppling her to the floor as quick as a flash of lightning.

She lost her grip on the gun and he kicked it inside the elevator before the door closed, then brought his hands to her throat.

"Nice scar," he growled under his breath. "Someone else's mistake is my gain, sweet sparrow." Underneath his ski mask he wore a translucent plastic mask covering his features except for the slits in place of eyes but it was hard to tell eye color. His hateful statement threw her off her game as flashes of Renner with his shiny blade flooded in as if it was happening this very moment, all over again.

Fear raced through her blood leaving an arctic wake.

Do something! Move!

She lifted her torso slightly then headbutted her attacker, forcing him to release his grip and fall to the side. Libby kneed him in the groin then jumped to her feet as he groaned, and raced toward the stairwell. She jerked the handle, but it wouldn't budge.

He must have jammed it from the other side.

The Eye stood in the middle of the hall as if no one would see or hear them, as if they had all the time in the world. To get to the elevator, she had to run past him.

She was trapped, and the hunting knife in his right hand glinted. Renner Ragsdale filled her mind. Coming for her. Shoving her down. She'd tried to make sure Lucas and the First Lady were safe and he'd gotten the jump on her, quickly slicing into her throat as she pressed the emergency button on her wrist to call in reinforcements and the ambulance.

Sweat drenched her back and face. Behind her was a small stairwell then the door to the roof.

The Eye stalked toward her. Her heart pounded as she froze in place. Phantom pains along her neck ached and her throat throbbed. She bolted for the door to the roof, thankful it opened. She hurried and set off the emergency app on her phone. Axel would track her and come to her aid, but until then she was on her own.

Just her. And the man who wanted to butcher her.

She raced up the six stairs and onto the roof, which overlooked downtown. Building after building stacked next to each other. She slammed the door and snatched a patio table with an ashtray full of cigarette butts. She tossed it in front of the door to slow The Eye down and began searching for a place to hide until Axel appeared.

The door burst open, the patio table tumbling over. The Eye sprinted for her, and she raced across the flat concrete surface, but she had nowhere to hide.

She never should have come up here. Everyone knew to run down, not up. Up was like being backed into a corner, and she was. A little mouse with no place to scurry.

Libby made an abrupt halt, bracing herself for his impact. She wasn't sure she could fight even though she knew how. Fear was screaming in her ear, reminding her she was going to die, and if Axel did make it to the roof in time, she might have to watch him die too, as she had Lucas.

The Eye smacked against her, and his knife

slipped from his hand. She quickly kicked it several feet away. Libby could not let him get that blade in his hands or she might be done for.

He grabbed her ankle and yanked her down with him, her side taking the brunt and knocking the air from her lungs. He scrambled to his feet with a grunt. Libby had hurt him and used it as an advantage, aiming her fist into his broken or bruised ribs. His venomous yelp pierced the air and he hurled insults at her and slammed a fist into her face. Stars burst in her eyes, blurring her vision.

No. She could not pass out, but nausea and black dots swept over her.

Run, Libby! Don't lay here helpless. You are not helpless.

But run where?

As his hands descended on her throat, she grabbed them, yanking him toward her, not away, then used her feet to springboard against his chest. The momentum did as she intended and flung him over her head. He landed on his back with a thud, and she jumped to her feet, dizzy but able to see.

The building next door was only about eight feet away.

But twenty stories up.

The Eye was already on his feet, blocking her path to the door back inside. She had to grab the knife, though it intensified her nausea.

Libby dove for the blade, but he was faster, snatching it and slicing her arm. The sting stole her breath, but adrenaline was pumping and she bolted across the roof preparing to jump the eight feet to the other building. She had the prowess, athleticism and she did CrossFit. She could jump. She could do this. She had to do this.

Time to go.

She hunched forward and increased her speed to gain the momentum she needed to spring off the roof's ledge. If she didn't clear the building, she would be dead. Plain and simple.

As she raced closer to the edge, flashbacks of her near-death experience blared in living color. Lucas being ripped open by the blade, their future bleeding out like the both of them. Renner Ragsdale, stalking toward her to watch her life drain before running into the night.

She was almost at the ledge.

Two more feet.

Sweat had cemented her shirt to her back. Her heart pounded like a bass drum in her ears. A knot grew in her throat.

The knife slicing through her skin. The shock. The fear.

She placed her dominant foot on the ledge, ready to spring. She pushed off.

And felt the snag of her other foot.

He had her but let her go…and it had slowed down her jump.

The Eye intended it. But why? His MO was stabbing. What kind of game was he playing?
Panic struck her heart as clarity dawned. She wasn't going to make it.

SIX

Axel finished clearing his section of the floors. Nothing suspicious but that didn't mean a killer wasn't hiding out and blending in. Anyone could steal a badge and enter the building. The Eye was someone who blended in well with the average Joe. He could be here now under Axel's nose, and he had to admit that was unnerving to say the least. He led Harley into his office as his phone alerted him with shrill beeping.

911 911 911

Libby was in trouble. No wonder she hadn't replied to his earlier text that all on his end was clear. "Lock the door and do not let a single person in. I have an emergency."

"What's going on?"

Axel bolted from the room. "Lock the door! Now."

Axel's heart accelerated like a NASCAR driver on the last loop on the inside. Blood whooshed in his ears and adrenaline sped through his veins.

Axel opened his tracking app on his watch, his fingers trembling. Every second was a second Libby might be dying.

A red dot with her name came into view. She wasn't in the building at all. She was next door. Why would she be in the building next to them? Had she been in pursuit? No, Libby would have checked this floor and then gone up before coming back down. Which meant she'd been on the roof.

His knees turned weak and his stomach bottomed out. He sprinted for the elevator and hit the button, but it was taking too long. He ran for the stairs and took them three at a time until he reached the top floor. It had been barricaded by some kind of long steel spike. Panic flooded him as he removed it and rushed onto the floor. Turning to the right, he saw the door open that led to the roof. She wouldn't have left it open unless someone was already behind her.

Bile rose in his throat. He hurdled all six stairs that led to the roof and into the spring sunshine. In case The Eye was on the roof still, he didn't call out her name. But she wasn't in this building anyway. He feared the worst. She'd been thrown over the top of the roof and landed in the vicinity of the next building. Axel kept to the big and bulky chimney system and darted past an outdoor shed.

He didn't have to worry about looking down and seeing a broken and bloody Libby. She hung off the roof ledge of the next building, oscillating her legs like a pendulum to gain momentum to swing them upward and over the ledge but that was far too risky. She could lose her grasp at any moment.

Axel hollered, "Stop! Stop now! Just focus on hanging on or you'll risk plummeting." His pulse thundered in his ears. Her grasp was not solid. How long had she been holding on for dear life?

"Axel! I—I—don't know how much longer I've got."

Libby's frantic and petrified words turned his blood ice cold. He backed up about ten feet, no time for any other option.

Libby would be dead.

For all he knew, the killer was on his way up to the rooftop next door to kick her off the ledge she hung from.

Without another thought, Axel sprinted the ten feet and sprang off the ledge, clearing the building and landing on the opposite rooftop, falling and rolling. He scrambled to his feet.

"Axel! I'm losing it! I'm losing my grip!" she shrieked.

He raced to the ledge just as her hands slid off the ledge and a bloodcurdling cry escaped her lungs.

Axel plunged his arms out, straining over the rooftop ledge and grabbed ahold of her right wrist in midair, his stitched wound burning. Libby wasn't light as a feather. She was built like a solid brick house made of pure muscle and only a few inches shy of six feet. Her frantic blue eyes met his; sweat poured from her brow, soaking the hair around her temples that had come loose from her ponytail.

His heart broke at the fear pulsing behind them. "I've got you, hon. You aren't going anywhere. You hear me?"

She nodded and glanced down the twenty stories—280 feet below—and a quivering moan escaped her lips.

"Libs, look at me." He had already dug in his heels along the concrete ledge's lip to anchor himself, otherwise they both might tumble over. "I. Have. You."

"You have me," she said through a crack in her voice. "You have me," she said more confidently as she peered into his eyes, and he spotted deep trust behind her fear.

He pulled her up with both of his arms, needing all his strength as his muscles spasmed and sweat dripped into his eyes. But he never stopped holding her eye contact. He needed her to see he was going to stand by his word and save her. He had the might to do it.

Slowly the fear dissipated and faith stared back at him. Faith in his word. Faith in his ability. "You're going nowhere but right to me."

Libby nodded as he finished pulling her over the ledge and into his arms, the weight and release sending them tumbling backward.

But she was safe.

She collapsed on him and her sigh of relief turned into tears. He'd only seen Libby tear up once when she told him about Lucas and how he'd died. Now, Axel held her against him, stroking her hair.

His heart still jackhammered in his chest. He had almost lost his best friend. A few seconds later, and they might not be sitting safely on a roof.

Axel sat up, shifting Libby into his lap, and he cradled her, her arms around his neck like a vise and her tears soaking his neck.

"Thank you, Axel."

His embrace tightened, cocooning her into him. "You're safe. You're always safe with me, Libby." He hoped that was true. He wanted it to be true.

Libby finally released her death grip on him and pulled back to look into his face. Placing her hands on his cheeks, she kissed him dead on his mouth. Not intimate or revealing, or even tender, but it shifted his heart a little and spiked his finally slowing heart rate.

She released his face and her cheeks reddened as her eyes turned to saucers. Looked like she'd surprised herself by kissing him and now she was embarrassed.

"That was so unprofessional of me." Yet she hadn't made a move from his lap.

"I'll write you up for it tomorrow," he teased.

Finally, her shoulders relaxed and she collapsed on his shoulder with a shuddering breath. "I'm just so happy to be alive. I would have kissed anyone who saved me."

"Is that so? Next time, I'll let someone else do it. And maybe he'll have halitosis." He kidded around, but the thought of her kissing anyone else needled him.

She laughed and tousled his hair. "What would I do without you?" She stood on wobbly legs and he followed suit, brushing dirt from his jeans.

"Fall off a roof," he said.

She gave him the stink eye. "Too soon, pal."

He tucked a strand of hair that had come loose behind her ear. "So you wanna jump back across or take the elevator down? I can make it. Can't say the same for you."

Libby jutted her sharp but slightly square chin. "I take back all the nice things I said about you. Ever."

"You've threatened this before, and if you recall, I responded with, 'no take backs.'" He opened the door from the roof to the inner building, which seemingly remained unlocked for employees to come and go for breaks.

Libby entered the elevator first and glanced back at him. "I recall nothing of that conversation." She undid her ponytail and regathered it, including the stray hairs—and the one he'd tucked—before redoing it.

"It was implied."

"Not the same." She hit the elevator button, and they rode down in silence.

Their little banter bit was light, but they both knew it was masking fear and anxiety, the gravity of having just almost died. It was their way. Axel's mind was a whir of thoughts and his heart a myriad of emotions: terror, relief, anger that someone had attacked her, and she had to hang from a roof for her life. And another emotion that was warm and pushing out the icy anxious thoughts. Libby hadn't been romantic in that kiss, but it had conjured emotions that he'd never noticed. Or feelings he might have noticed but ignored; it was a little harder to ignore a kiss.

He was going to do his best to try. Instead of allowing those thoughts, he would think about The Eye and the fury he felt toward him at this moment. Axel rescued Libby this time, and it had felt good to have someone believe in him when he'd lost faith in himself. It was humbling to know he was her safe space and held her trust.

But what if he failed her next time? What if he wasn't there when The Eye struck again, like with Cheryl? The only way to protect Libby was to never leave her side for a second, but that was pretty much impossible.

"He called me sweet sparrow, Axel."

She confirmed what he already knew in his gut.

"I just don't fit the profile for his victims." She shook her head and rubbed the back of her neck.

"Me. It's my fault like I said earlier. I left the FBI, and to him that meant ignoring and turning my back on him. Targeting you in a myriad of ways returns me to him and forces me to think about him—as if I already don't. He wants to remind me that he can take anyone I care about, like he robbed me of Cheryl, and at any time and in any manner. He's veering from his normal MO and that's the only explanation I can offer as to why."

"Well, why didn't he choose Amber? Y'all are tight," she said with a frown.

Good question, and it pushed Axel to think about Libby and their friendship. "Amber and I are friends. She's like a little sister to me." He paused as he faced the truth that he and Libby went far beyond that to a deeper relationship. "It's...not the same with us."

Tension filled the elevator. "I just mean—"

"I know what you mean," she said. "We spend a lot of time off-duty together, and you and she don't. Why is that?"

He wasn't sure. Amber was an incredible woman and a tough protector. She'd even endured a heavy loss like he and Libby. They had that in common. But he and Libby had just clicked in a way he and Amber hadn't.

The elevator door opened before he had to answer, and he didn't really have one—or at least not an answer he was willing to give. That would require spending time with his feelings. Not happening.

Instead, they walked next door and entered Harley's building. "No alert from Harley, so let's assume he's safe. Then we can access security footage from the building. See if we can find The Eye."

"He wore a cheap plastic mask—you know, the kind with red lips, rosy cheeks against a translucent background. His features were hidden but his eyes might be dark behind those slits. I know they're cold and full of venom and hate." Libby shuddered. "He's taller than me but not by much. I'd say he's six-one or -two."

"Good intel." He hit the elevator button to the

nineteenth floor. "We won't be able to gain facial recognition, but we might see him leave the building and whether he got into a car like an Uber or cab or his own."

"Feels like grasping at straws."

"I'll grasp whatever I can." Axel and Libby rode the rest of the way in silence. The elevator opened to Harley's floor, and she took Axel's forearm, halting him from exiting.

"Thanks again for grasping *me*. For real. Axel..." Her voice broke. "I haven't felt that helpless and hopeless since the night I almost died and Lucas did. It's a wonder I'm here already, and that I can even speak at all."

"Sometimes I wish you couldn't," he teased, avoiding the tough topic. Normally, he didn't shy away from conflict or confronting emotions, but for some reason, he couldn't go there right now. Maybe not ever. This was getting too intense between them.

"You're a real comedian, Axel." She shoved him as they stepped off the elevator then they resumed professional statures.

He paused. Making light was the wrong thing to do. She had been vulnerable with him. Now, he took her hand. "I'm sorry it brought back traumatic memories. I really am."

She squeezed his hand. "I know. Thank you."

After staring at each other a few moments,

they returned to Harley's office. A little brunette in her mid to late twenties stood at the desk outside. "He's not answering calls or his door."

"He will for me." Axel went through the mental checklist. This wasn't the blonde who was Harley's admin assistant. Macy Davis. "But has anyone else tried that you know about?"

She shook her head. "No. I stepped in for Macy. She took a coffee break. No one has been by since I've been here."

"And you are?" Libby asked.

"Angie Wolcott. I'm just here to relieve Macy. Mr. Coburn gets angry if he's interrupted by someone without an appointment, so she asked me to standby in case someone showed up while she took a break."

She wore a badge and seemed legit, and now scared. "Has something happened to him? A memo went out that a private security detail would be with him today due to the threats."

"I'm sure he's fine. Thank you." Axel knocked on Harley's door. "It's Axel, Harley. Safe to open up."

But Harley didn't answer.

Axel looked at Libby, and she mirrored his grim expression. "Did you arrive before or after Macy took her break?" Axel asked.

Her cheeks reddened. "Sorry. It was just a few minutes after. No more than ten. Why? What's wrong? Did I do something wrong?"

Maybe. Maybe not. Axel turned the knob. Unlocked.

Where was Harley?

Libby had no time to process her near-death experience—for the second time in her life. Right now, the man they'd been paid a hefty fee to protect was missing. Had the killer used her to get to Harley?

Why? Many times serial killers became furious when their "work" was accredited to someone else. Right now, Harley Coburn was the poster boy for The Eye's killings. He might not like sharing the limelight. Maybe The Eye wanted to kill her to hurt Axel and make him pay for walking away from him and to kill Harley to prove law enforcement of every branch had it wrong.

"I'll check the men's room," Axel said. "Last ditch effort, but we can't not look just because he has his own private bath. You look in the lounge area. He didn't set off his emergency alarm so maybe it's nothing." Axel's mouth was pursed and his jaw ticked. "In which case I'm going to be very displeased."

Libby pulled a "yikes" face. Axel angry was never a pretty sight. She rushed in the opposite direction toward the lounge. Her body still quaked from adrenaline, and her pulse continued to race. She entered the lounge to three middle-aged women drinking coffee and indulging in blueberry scones, which on any other occasion would make her mouth water.

"Did any of you see Harley Coburn in the past ten to fifteen minutes?"

The bottle blonde spoke up. "I haven't seen him since he went into his office. Wish I saw more of him," she teased, and the other two ladies tittered and playfully slapped her arms. She was aware that Harley was good-looking as well as charming. Didn't seem like they believed the rumors going around about him being a killer.

She left the lounge, peeping into offices and being shot with scowls and surprised expressions.

No Harley.

As she turned the corner two doors down from his office, a door swung open nearly smacking her upside the head. Libby had always had quick reflexes and they'd come in handy just now. "Excuse you," she said, and then Harley appeared with an apologetic expression.

"Oh, I'm sorry."

She sighed, thankful he hadn't been kidnapped or killed but once she was sure he was okay, annoyance took charge. He'd potentially risked his life. "Why are you out of your office when Axel specifically said to stay inside until he gave you permission?"

He opened his mouth to speak but Libby cut him off. "When he tells you things like that, you need to heed them. We can't do our jobs if you decide to be reckless and ignore our instructions. They're for your safety. You put your life, potentially others and ours in danger."

She flashed back to the roof when she'd frozen like a scared puppy. Couldn't fight back because fear had overtaken her. Anger bubbled to the surface—at herself. "No matter how much training and skill you possess, you are not invincible!" She'd been bested. Hadn't even used a quarter of the defense tactics she'd been trained in to fight back.

"Hey," Axel said as he approached, his voice gentle. "I see you found Mr. Coburn."

Harley slipped out of the large closet as big as an office, closing the door behind him, his expression confused and also caught. "I'm sorry. I was out of…toilet paper. I wasn't sure how long you'd be gone and Macy was gone on break when I needed it." He held up a roll with a sheepish grin.

Axel looked at Libby and she rolled her eyes.

"You couldn't have waited until Angie relieved her?" Axel said.

Harley shrugged. "Look, I'm sorry and I didn't mean to be gone that long, but I couldn't find any on the shelves in here and had to dig through a bunch of boxes."

"Well, go on back to your office. We'll discuss it further," Axel said.

"Has the building been breached?" Harley asked, like he was in a war movie.

"We'll discuss this in private. Just go straight to the office and stay there. Do not stand or get near your windows. We'll be right along," Axel said.

Harley nodded and scurried down the hall toward his office, then they watched him enter, shut the heavy wooden door, making a raucous display of locking it.

"Toilet paper? Really?" Axel asked.

"Lame. But would we have wanted him to hit the emergency button for that?" Libby asked. She'd seen clients ignore them for far less than a roll of Charmin.

"No." Axel sighed. "Let's talk about that little gasket you blew on him."

Libby inwardly cringed. She had been pretty over-the-top. "I'm sorry."

"I know. You have every reason to be on edge, but I'm not talking about unprofessionalism with a client, Libs. I want to talk about the fact you're mad at yourself because you didn't necessarily win this match, and you projected that anger at yourself onto our client who messed up for a roll of toilet paper." He gripped both of her shoulders.

"You aren't perfect. You're human, and we don't always sense danger or see a scuffle coming."

Axel was right, but he ought to swallow his own advice. Instead of pointing that out and hurting him or starting a real fight, she'd let it pass. Axel could no more have known The Eye was setting him up to leave for Dallas than anyone else on that FBI task force.

"Axel, I'm not mad because I'm not perfect. Though I am pretty close," she teased to lighten the heaviness about to come from her. But he didn't bite or banter back.

He drilled into her gaze with a soberness that wouldn't let her off the hook with humor.

Fine. She'd be honest, and if he wanted to remove her from the case or the job, then it was what it was. "I'm not angry over my lack of skill getting me into trouble. I'm angry over my fear. I froze up there. Not for long, but time enough for him to catch my leg. I wasn't afraid of jumping. I can clear eight to ten feet and I'm not afraid to die. To be absent in body is to be present with God. I was afraid of—"

"The pain. The way you might be ended," he murmured.

"Yes." Tears burned the backs of her eyes. "I kept feeling that blade he held along my throat, and it threw me back into the past." She touched her scar at her neck. "That fear made me hesitate, giving him time to slow down my jump."

He turned the knob on the supply closet and held it, gazing into her eyes, then he pushed it open and hauled her inside the spacious, dark room filled with rows of metal cabinets loaded with supplies, boxes and an old copy machine in the corner. Her eyes adjusted further to see him staring right at her, his large frame looming. Axel drew her to his chest and enveloped her.

He didn't need to say anything, and Libby didn't want him to. Instead, she received what Axel was offering and she desperately needed—a warm, safe place that allowed her to feel secure. Axel's chest wasn't soft but solid, and she inhaled his understated cologne, a mix of spicy and cool.

Libby wrapped her arms around his waist and clung to him, clung to the refuge he'd become for her, to the feeling rolling off him in waves reassuring her that she didn't need to be afraid or anxious for anything even in the darkness. He was light, casting a soft glow of hope around her weary soul.

"I almost died," she whispered, knowing she was stating the obvious but needing to say it until it didn't petrify her anymore. "I hung from a building and almost died." She said it again as a few hot tears surfaced and spilled down her cheeks.

His lips rested in her hair as he drew her farther into him until she wasn't sure where she ended and he began.

"Axel, you jumped a building for me. Did you pop your stitches?"

"No. Just strained them. I'm sore but fine."

"Okay, but you could have slipped or..." She pulled back at the weight of that thought, her nose inches from his. His cool minty breath slid into her nostrils. He could have died because of her. Lucas died because of her. "Would you have done that for Amber, Bridge or Archer?" she murmured.

His hands framed her face. "I would have but..."

"But?"

His inhale was deep. "But nothing I guess," he whispered, the tip of his straight nose touching hers.

He guessed? What did that mean? Were his feelings of friendship toward her progressing into whatever "nothing I guess" meant? The idea terrified her. Love guided reckless behavior. That's what got Lucas killed. She never wanted to be the reason Axel died or was injured, and yet she already was. He had six stitches to prove it.

They were too close. Not only physically at this moment, but their heart strings—or at least hers—were growing tangled, and she needed headspace as much as she needed physical space.

"Good. If our friendship keeps us from clear thinking or muddles our ability, then we have to rethink things." She cleared her throat and straightened her shoulders, raising an invisible barrier that not only guarded her heart but would help keep Axel's safe too, just in case.

Axel's cheek twitched, but he nodded once and followed Libby out of the closet. As she closed the door, she thought she heard something inside the closet and the idea of a rodent gave her the willies. She followed Axel to Harley's office where he sat behind his desk with a cup of coffee.

When he saw them, he raised it. "I buzzed Angie to bring it to me. Never left."

"Good," Libby said. "I want to apologize for jumping on you. We did have a breach. In full disclosure you need to know that I was attacked on the twentieth floor by someone who we believe is the real Eye. I had to jump to the next building to escape."

A noise drew their attention, and another young woman in her mid-to late twenties stood gaping. Blond with bright green eyes. "I'm sorry. I didn't mean to interrupt." She held up a file folder. "Mr. Coburn, you asked for this."

"Of course, Macy. Thanks."

She walked to his desk, her perfume leaving a flowery trail in her wake. She handed him the folder and lingered a little longer than an admin assistant should. Another woman slobbering over Harley Coburn or hoping to hear some of their spilled tea?

"Could you keep quiet about what you heard?" Axel asked her. "We wouldn't want to cause a panic, and everything is clearly fine."

She blinked up at him, her eyes widening and her pupils dilating. So she was attracted to everyone then. But the way she looked at Axel got a rise out of Libby that didn't happen when the woman's attention was on Harley. "Of course. I know how to be discreet." She cast another glance at Harley. "If you need me, Mr. Coburn, you know where to find me."

He nodded and she left. Axel closed the door and waited a beat. Sometimes big ears didn't exit right away.

"Macy Davis is a gem, and she knows how to be discreet. No worries." Harley set his cup on the desk with a clunk. "Back to what you said a second ago. You jumped a building?"

"It wasn't as glamorous as the movies make it." She nearly died, but she decided to keep that to herself. No point seeming incompetent to Harley. She wasn't.

But she might be. Fear had stabbed hooks into her, holding her back from fighting when she could have taken him down. She'd failed. Libby had spent a year in therapy working through the trauma, and her therapist told her she would have PTSD, and it would often hit when she least expected it. Libby admitted to panic attacks and some anxiety. She'd never hesitated before, though. Not like this. Maybe because she'd never had a serial killer set his sights on her—the same one who'd butchered Axel's wife. Libby had seen the crime photos. Read the case files. It was gruesome. Macabre.

"I didn't mean it like that. I meant… I'm just stunned. Was it someone who was after me—like were they trying to kill you to get to me?" His pulse ticked in his throat.

At first they thought so, but seeing Harley in the closet of his own accord changed their minds. "I don't believe so. You continue to be safe with us. We do need to make a few private calls, though."

"We'll be right outside," Axel said, and they left his office and went into the empty office next door. They called Archer on speakerphone and updated him on the earlier event.

Archer reacted as Libby suspected. Concern over her well-being and mental health. She confirmed she was perfectly fine, but the truth was she wasn't fine at all.

Archer then sighed and cleared his throat. "I know that Coburn trusts us even with someone targeting you, Libby—let's thank God we have location trackers on our Locale App on our phones. There's a measure of safety in knowing where you are. But while you were hanging from a roof, someone could have swooped in and taken our client or killed him, especially with a ten minute gap between admin assistants at their desk. I've already had security footage pulled. Whoever attacked you must have stolen a badge or had one made. Not sure, but nothing suspicious and sadly the camera to the roof was disabled. We're looking at a great hacker, or someone on Security might have been bribed. I'll have Bridge handle those interviews but I'm not expecting much. They could say it's a glitch and we have no proof otherwise. We did clock a man leaving the building around the time you'd have jumped from one roof to another, but his face never turned toward the cameras and he wore a fedora, so he knew the layout."

Libby remained silent. Discovering her attacker was pretty much nil, and Archer had a valid point. She braced herself for the other bad news coming.

"I think it's wise to pull you from protection duty, and Axel will watch your back. You can take the investigation from Bridge and Amber into who might be trying to kill Harley, and they can guard Coburn. I'll have Bridge call the FBI and report the new developments concerning The Eye so they can investigate on their end."

"I can keep Harley safe," Libby insisted.

"This has nothing to do with your capabilities, Libby. We wouldn't have asked you to come on board if we thought you didn't have the moxie to do this job. This is about a serious killer coming after you. You need to focus on that."

Libby would have made the same call if she was in Archer's position, and Archer didn't know that Libby had hesitated. If Harley had been on the roof with her, he could have died. "Okay."

"I'll send them over STAT. And guys, good work. You're irreplaceable, Libby. I don't know anyone who can swing like you."

"I took a hit from her and I'm still alive," Axel teased.

"Because I let you remain standing." Why hadn't she fought The Eye to the end? Pounded him to bits?

Fear.

Maybe she was no longer cut out for this job or any other involved in protecting others. If Archer knew she'd hesitated and froze, he might change his mind on how irreplaceable she was.

"Once Amber and Bridge arrive, we'll let Harley know about the changes," Axel said. "Be easier after he has the chance to speak with them in person."

They ended the call after a few more moments of conversation then returned to Harley's office.

"Everything okay?"

"It is," Axel said.

"Can I use your restroom?" Libby asked. Her cheeks were on fire, and she could use some cold water on them. Since her near-death experience, Libby hadn't had a single moment to process it alone, and she needed space.

"Sure. Right in there." He pointed to the bathroom and she entered. Running the water ice cold, she splashed it on her face, cooling her flushed cheeks and washing away the salty film of sweat. Her scar caught her eye as it always did. The constant reminder of mortality and loss. After patting her face dry with a hand towel, she noticed the stainless-steel toilet paper holder on the floor by the sink.

It was full. Six rolls.

When Harley left the closet, he only had one roll in his hand.

What had he actually been doing in that supply closet? And why had he been lying?

SEVEN

Axel stood near the bougie coffee bar, but he wasn't complaining because it made excellent espresso. He sipped his drink and kept a nonchalant stance, but he was keeping an eagle eye out for any kind of trouble, particularly from The Eye.

Axel fully believed that targeting Libby was a jab at him. She didn't fit the killer's type by not being in the medical field. And if he had targeted her, it would have been before they took on Harley Coburn's case since Libs had been stalked for over a month.

This vicious monster must have been keeping tabs on Axel for the past five years, noticing the closeness between him and Libby. Now he was using it to bait Axel into the game again—the hunt. But this was no game to Axel. People he deeply cared about had died. Now Libby had been attacked and removed from protective duty. She understood, but having Axel declared officially as her own private bodyguard—though Archer had put it more delicately—would irritate her to no end and he understood that too. Axel would have felt the same way if he were in her shoes.

Libby was strong, independent and tough. Those traits didn't make for a good client.

And what happened in the supply closet?

Libby's vulnerability had moved him, and he'd come close to crossing a line in their friendship by wanting to kiss her, by almost doing it. What was going on with him? From inhaling that perfume on her vanity to his actions in the closet, things were a mess in his heart and head. But the thought of that perfume behind her ears, on her wrists...he needed to rein his thoughts in and destroy them before he destroyed their friendship. Libs had made that perfectly clear.

He didn't want things to change between them. They had the perfect setup. So why was he wanting to inhale perfume on her body and kiss her? Granted, when he'd first met her he thought she was stunning and immediately felt guilt. Cheryl had only been gone a year when Libby came to work for Spears & Bow. But the attraction was undeniable. And they shared the same kind of dark humor, enjoyed the same shows and sports. They'd both lost their loved ones, and the connection grew until they'd become the best of friends. Their relationship was deep and abiding. But he'd never allowed himself to think past the fact she was incredibly beautiful—even the scar that revealed her bravery, courage and will to survive.

Now things were going sideways, and he had no idea why or how to fix it back to the way it used to be. Axel returned with his espresso to Harley's office and settled in a chair by the window.

"We hear y'all just been hanging around today," Bridge said as he entered the office with Amber Rathbone. She was petite but a firecracker, with dark brown hair that hung all one length below her chin. Her gray eyes met Bridge's and she snorted.

"Ha. Ha." Libby entered behind them and Amber hugged her.

"You good, girl?"

"I am. Now."

Bridge hugged her next and rustled the top of her head in a brotherly fashion. Married, and family life looked good on him.

"What's going on? Has the threat grown?" Harley asked. "Do I need all four of you guarding me now?"

"No, but the dynamics are changing," Axel said. "The real Eye has targeted Libby. It was him today on the roof, and this is both bad news and good news. Good news because it further supports you are not the killer and bad news because Libby will need to recuse herself from your case. I'll be leaving as well. We plan to work on who might be attacking you while Bridge and Amber will become your new bodyguards. You're in great hands."

Harley looked at each one of them then landed his sight on Axel. "If you think that's best. But so you know, I'm not worried about you and Ms. Winters failing to keep me safe even with someone, sadly, after her too."

"I appreciate that," Libby said. "But we need to focus on finding him and looking out for my safety, which would keep us from being thorough with yours, and we are always thorough."

Bridge and Amber agreed, and Amber stepped closer to Harley. "We'll make sure you're safe, Mr. Coburn. We're following up with the men that attacked you and other leads. So we could be out of your hair sooner than later. I'm sure you're ready to have some freedom back."

He smirked.

Bridge showed him his watch. "We have the emergency app as well, so if you set it off we'll also hear and see it. Nothing changes there."

"We'll step next door and review some logistics then take over," Amber said. She had a warm and disarming smile that made her dangerous. Axel and Archer had really loved that about her, but women often tended to feel safer with Libby due to her no-nonsense approach to safety. She was kind, but she had a face that let a person know she could kill them if they touched her. The team's skills were all diverse, and he and Archer had picked each of them for those reasons.

They entered the small, empty office next to Harley's.

"Feel like flying to Dallas?" Bridge asked.

"Who's in Dallas?" Libby asked.

Flying away would keep Libby safer than being here in the clutches of The Eye. Axel wasn't opposed to that at all. He'd love to whisk her somewhere away from civilization and leave it to Archer and the rest of the team to find this monster. But unfortunately that wasn't feasible, and Libby wouldn't run with no clear-cut plan to return. It wasn't her style, and while he hated she wouldn't, it was one of the qualities he loved most in her—tenacity and fortitude.

"We have a lead. Joel Wickham. His wife was The Eye's ninth victim. Her name was Hilary and she was a nurse at Methodist Dallas. She'd been six weeks pregnant and hadn't even known according to Joel. When Harley was taken into custody for questioning, Wickham made a big production and even threatened to kill him if he ever had the chance. According to Wickham, Harley had eaten lunch with Hilary two days before she died. In Harley's police interview, he said that they were friends. That's all. She'd been a friend of his sister's in school and moved to Dallas. They were simply catching up."

"What do you think about that answer?" Axel asked, feeling somewhat skeptical himself.

Bridge raked his hand through his hair. "I think Wickham suspects Coburn and his late wife may have had an affair, and that's enough to drive a person to murder. Seen it before."

They probably all had since they'd come from law enforcement backgrounds.

"Was Coburn questioned about an affair with Hilary Wickham any further?" Axel asked.

Amber tucked a bang behind her ear. "Nothing in the reports to indicate they questioned him further, and the paternity test showed Joel was the father. I guess they didn't think they needed to."

"Would Harley cop to it? An affair?" Libby asked.

Axel had done a lot of profiling work with the Bureau even though he wasn't ever a part of its Behavioral Analysis Unit. "He's been upfront so far, and if it's true he has nothing to lose as it might stop the attacks on him, providing Wickham is our guy."

"Worth a shot," Bridge said. "Since you two have already established rapport, it might be best if you ask. Which one of you would he be more apt to confide in?"

"You mean who would he perceive as less judgy? Libby." Since Axel had been married previously, Coburn might assume he was more judgmental of affairs than a single woman who had never been married. "Coburn is charming and women like him. I'd send her in."

"I'll go now." Libby headed for Harley's office and his listening device on his watch signaled. Libby was going to let them listen in on the app that substituted for an ear wig with a mic.

"Oh, hey Libby," Harley said. "Everything okay?"

"Yeah. Can I have a seat on your couch?"

"Of course."

"I want to talk to you about something a little sensitive that's come up in our investigation. We may have a viable person of interest in the attempts on your life. So your cooperation will not only help us catch this man but might lift the heat from you."

"Okay," Harley said warily. "What is it you'd like to know?"

"Hilary Wickham. Can you tell me about your relationship with her?" Libby asked, her tone even, calm. No hint of judgment or criticism in it.

"I sometimes had meetings with doctors and other personnel at the hospital. She was the charge nurse in oncology. She was a friend. We had lunch sometimes together." His voice was as even and honest as Libby's.

"Did it maybe go beyond a platonic relationship? More intimate?"

Harley didn't speak for a few moments. "You want to know if we had an affair."

"I do. Joel Wickham may be exacting revenge on you and using vigilante justice as his cover."

"Ah." Harley inhaled deeply. "We grew close. A few dinners. It moved in a direction we didn't expect."

"So you did have an affair?"

"No. Yes." He sounded flustered. "Emotional yes. Truth is we were falling in love, but she died before it ever turned physical. If she hadn't died, I think she would have left Joel regardless of me. They were having problems before I met her."

"Do you think Joel knew this prior to hearing it from the police—about the lunch two days before she died?" Libby asked.

"I don't think so. But I can't say for sure. I never knew Joel."

"Harley, your honesty is going to help us so much. We won't divulge this, as it's not necessary. It would only cement in the vigilante's eyes that you're guilty."

Axel looked at Bridge and Amber. "If the killings weren't perfectly identical each time, I might be inclined to believe that Wickham killed his wife and framed The Eye, but she had the hymn stabbed into her chest. How would he know that? He wouldn't." He answered his own question.

"If Wickham had friends at the PD, someone

could have let something slip. Check into that," Amber said.

Axel nodded. "We will. We'll head to Dallas tomorrow afternoon. We'll talk to more than Joel Wickham. There are other victims' families still in that area we won't rule out."

Bridge grinned. "And extend Libby's time far from El Paso. I know how you're thinking. I'd be thinking the same thing."

Libby entered the room. "I believe him."

"I do too," Axel said. "Let's head to the office, get what we need and then we'll figure out where we're staying tonight."

Libby's lips pursed, but she dipped her chin in acknowledgment. "See you two tomorrow morning. Maybe."

"Maybe," Amber said. "Keep yourself safe and use Goliath there to watch your back." She winked and giggled when Libby rolled her eyes.

"I could use his eyes behind my back. But I can take care of myself, and he's big but I can drop him."

"Back to that again, huh?" Axel said. "Keep talking, woman. That's all it is." He grinned and opened the door, allowing her to exit first. "You know so I can keep my eyes on your back."

As they walked to the SUV, Axel paused, sensing eyes on them. A gut warning. And he never ignored his gut.

"We're going to take a long way around the mountain. See if we can flush out whoever's watching us."

Libby let out a soft breath but he heard the shakiness in it. He didn't point it out. She had every reason to be afraid and to keep up the brave facade. "I'll be watching too."

If only it would remain two people watching. But The Eye was clever, and he wouldn't stay in the shadows for long.

Libby kept an eye on the passenger-side mirror. Traffic was congested, but she hadn't noticed a tail; that didn't mean they weren't being followed. Inside, her nerves jumped and jerked, but there was something else that was bugging her. "Axel, I want to talk about the supply closet earlier."

His Adam's apple bobbed. "I'm not letting our friendship affect our work relationship. You know where I stand on the whole romance thing, and we work because you stand there too. I'm not in love with you, Libby. I do care about you like I care about everyone on our team. I don't want to see anyone hurt—or dead. So can we just not rehash the weird moment?"

Libby stiffened. Not what she was going to bring up. She didn't want Axel to fall for her, but hearing the confidence in his voice as he declared he was anything but in love with her stung—

probably just her ego. A platonic friendship that didn't slip over the line was what she wanted too. Easy. But things felt anything but easy.

"I was going to say that Harley said he went into the supply closet for toilet paper and he left with one roll, which he snagged last minute. Like an afterthought. Because when I went into his bathroom, the toilet paper holder was full. Six rolls. Not to mention I thought I heard movement in there. I chalked it up to a mouse but now I'm second-guessing myself."

Axel's neck reddened. Good. He should be embarrassed bringing up what they'd already dealt with, and he'd been a little forceful in his tone, which she could have done without. "I'm sorry. You know, now that you say it I thought I smelled perfume in there but chalked it up to employees entering and exiting. He may have been in there with a woman."

"Why hide?"

Axel shrugged. "Maybe she's married or there's a policy on interoffice relationships."

"There should be one in every office. In my opinion."

"That only makes coworkers want to be together more. Forbidden love."

"You a closet romance reader?" she teased, keeping her eye on the mirror.

Axel snorted and changed lanes.

No one changed with them, but the unease never dissipated.

They made it to the office without discovering a tail, but Libby's gut said they had been followed.

"Let's run in and pick up the files Bridge and Amber were combing through so we can pick up where they left off." They jumped out of the vehicle and raced to the building, keeping an eye out, her gun in hand just in case; she would be ready.

But would she?

What if she hesitated again? It could cost her life and potentially Axel's if he was with her.

They returned to the SUV with a plastic file box under each arm and put them in the back seat.

"Let's take everything back to my place," Libby said. "We didn't have lunch and I'm starving. I grocery shopped, so guess what I have."

"Roast beef and provolone with hoagie rolls."

"You know it." Hot roast beef sandwiches were her favorite, and everyone on the team knew it.

"Sounds good." Axel hopped in the driver's side, and they carefully made their way to Libby's. Once inside, they cleared the rooms while Axel mumbled about her not having a security system.

Libby had a camera at the front door and if anyone approached, she would be notified on the app and could see and hear. However, if they sneaked into the backyard, like last night, they'd surprise her. No cameras. But no one knew that except her.

"Libby, you need better security, and you have the money to do it. I pay you well."

"Not everyone has a Fort Knox." She sighed and went to the kitchen. After washing her hands, she dug out the roast beef, provolone, spicy mustard and mayo for Axel. He grabbed paper plates, napkins and cans of fizzy water. When she first started drinking them, he'd tried one and told her it tasted like television snow. She'd laughed so hard at that. But then she bought the orange flavored ones, and he changed his tune. Or rather he was okay with drinking orange TV snow.

He opened her pantry. "Doritos or Lay's?"

"Yes."

"I like the way you think, Libs." He opened both bags, which she really only kept for him. Give her a brownie over salty snacks any day.

She toasted the hoagie buns in her air fryer then laid the cheese and beef on them, letting them melt. Once the sandwiches were ready, she carried their plates to the table where Axel was already at work digging through the file boxes, though he knew most of this information by heart.

"What are you thinking?" Libby asked, and cracked open her sparkling water.

"We've added Joel Wickham to the list beside Paul DeVries, who is at the top with the most threats and altercations. Next to him is Vinny Wallace and Josh Ramos as Harley stated earlier. I remember both of them from when I was on the case. Spouses of victims three and five. Hilary is new to me. She was number nine and nine through twelve was after I left. After Cheryl. But they're just leads. It could be anyone."

"True."

Axel held up a file. "While we're in Dallas, I'd also like to talk to another possible suspect after Harley. Jordan Jenkins's wife, Annabeth, was killed by The Eye three years ago, making her victim ten, and he as well as Joel both have traveling jobs, which could put them here in El Paso at the times of attacks on Harley. Not to mention, Jordan works for a rival pharma company and that's just interesting to me."

Libby nodded, bit into her sandwich and refrained from openly groaning. Best. Sandwich. Ever. "Was she also in the medical field like the other victims to date—minus Cheryl?"

Axel nodded. "Nurses. Admins. Doctors. Technicians. Which is why Harley Coburn was a good fit, but most offices receive samples from multiple pharma companies. Have any of those reps been questioned? We need to look into that, or the local PDs do, I mean. I keep forgetting I don't work this case anymore."

"Except you do. I've seen your war room." Axel kept a spare bedroom full of notes on the case and even had a murder board in there. He may not officially be on the hunt, but Axel had never truly stopped searching for who might be The Eye. "Who did you think it might be when you were working with the FBI?"

"I didn't know. Other than I suspected he was a travel nurse or some kind of medical rep. Athletic, agile. Able to blend into a setting without being noticed, but charming and good-looking enough to disarm a woman or even entice her. Harley didn't become a person of interest until the twelfth and most recent victim, Casey Rogers, was murdered in her home in El Paso. They'd dated a few times and when police brought him in as someone who might give them insight, they discovered he'd dated Raela Jenner, victim number four—but that didn't pop up on my radar. The relationship was casual and short and revealed just six months ago when Casey died and after he was also linked to Hilary. We already know he had an affair with Hilary Wickham."

"He's left-handed and our killer is right. And he's not ambidextrous that we know of. Could it be someone he works with who could be setting him up for the fall if it ever went sideways? The Eye is calculated, and I wouldn't put it past him. We should ask or look ourselves, see who else might have been in those facilities at the same time as Coburn. We might find him that way."

"I'd think the FBI would run that avenue

down," Axel said, and added potato chips to his sandwich for the crunch factor.

"Not everyone is as thorough as you, Axel. If they're thinking it's him and can't get enough for an arrest, then they might not be looking anywhere but angles that point to Coburn so they can charge him. I've even wondered if The Eye is coming after Harley and pretending to be a victim's loved one to throw off law enforcement."

He added more Doritos to his plate. "Why would the real killer want to murder Harley? He's the perfect fall guy. Killing him opens up space for agents to look elsewhere."

"True. But we're dealing with a psychopath with narcissism. Any glory that isn't assigned to him means he isn't receiving that glory. Pretending it's for justice keeps anyone from looking elsewhere." Libby finished off her sandwich and broke up a cheesy nacho chip, eating it slowly.

"You're right. You'd think you had some law enforcement background or something," he teased.

"Imagine that," she countered, and grinned. "So whoever is after Harley could be the real Eye, and that means we're dealing with one person and not two or more. But here's the thing, why toy with me? He never did that to the other victims. He got inside their homes, took things. Then he killed them. He didn't show up in public places to murder them. He didn't chase them onto rooftops."

"No." Axel pushed his plate away as if the statement stole his appetite. "No he didn't. You already know what I think is going on."

Libby shook her head. "This isn't your fault, Axel. I don't blame you. This is all him. If he wants to play games, then we need to play too. I'm not a mouse. You're not a mouse. We're big cats. Lions. And you do not mess with this pride. We need to stop running and playing defense. Take offense. We'll outmatch, outwit and outplay him. He's hiding in the police reports. Someone saw something, knows something—they just don't realize it and we know how to ask the right questions."

A sly grin spread across Axel's face. "I do love it when you're feisty toward someone other than me."

"It's just more fun when it's directed at you." She collected their plates and put them in the recycle bin. "What say you? We gonna do this or keep running like scared rabbits?" But she was scared. Maybe she could borrow from the "fake it until you make it" ideology. It might work in her favor.

Or get her killed.

"Last time I got aggressive, Cheryl died."

"I'm not Cheryl, Axel." Why couldn't he see that?

"I know."

Did he? "Then let's get offensive. Let's get aggressive."

"You're not going to break out with the cheer, are you?" He smirked but concern and a hint of fear shone in his eyes. He was trying to make light to hide his trepidation. She understood because she did the exact same thing.

She'd indulge him and raised her hands, making cheerleading motions. "Be aggressive. *B-E* aggressive. *B-E-A-G-G*—"

Axel pulled a face. "Okay, put the pom-poms down. We're not going to continue to simply react. We'll be proactive."

"Perfect. Let's pore over files." She grabbed one file box and Axel combed through the one he'd already been working on. After about four hours, Libby stretched. "You want pizza?"

"Always. Let's order. Double pepperoni with mushrooms and olives from Nonna's? Extra large?"

"Is it even a pizza if it's not from Nonna's?" Axel knew her favorite places, favorite foods. She also knew he'd pick off the olives because he hated them. "But it's always over an hour wait for delivery. I'll call and you go head over. It'll be quicker and I'm hungry."

"I'm not leaving you here alone."

She inhaled, holding it and counting slowly. Libby could admit she was afraid and she'd frozen on the roof. But she just said they had to be aggressive. Go on the offense. She could do her job. She would do her job. "Axel. You said you trusted me. You said you knew I wasn't Cheryl and that I could take care of myself. It's twenty-five minutes max from the time I call it in. Put your money where your mouth is and by that I mean you can pay for the pizza."

Axel opened his mouth to protest then massaged the back of his neck. "Lock all the doors. Keep your gun and phone close—"

"I'm not ten."

"No, you're not. Call it in. I'll head that way now." He paused but grabbed his wallet and keys and headed out the door. She locked it behind him and called in the pizza. Fifteen minutes. By the time he got there the food would be ready.

While he was gone, Libby straightened up the mess, called her sister, Cass—omitting the attacks in their conversation—while she unloaded and reloaded the dishwasher, then she made a pot of coffee so it would be ready after dinner when they went back to work.

"So you think you're having feelings for him?" Cass asked.

"No. I mean I don't know. Things have shifted. But I'm nipping it in the bud."

"You know, Axel is a catch. You're forty-one, and he's what? Forty-three? If you live to be eighty, that's a lot of life to live without having a partner."

"He is my partner, my platonic partner."

"Keep telling yourself that, sis. Axel is a good man. A godly man and he's drool-on-the-floor gorgeous. If you don't make a move, I might," she teased.

Libby didn't love that idea even though Cass was kidding. "I try not to think about his looks." She would drool. She didn't wear blinders.

"Look, I have to get ready. I'm on the night shift."

Cass worked for a shipping company and ran the late shift. "Okay. Axel should return in a few minutes." He'd been gone for nearly twenty-five minutes. She ended the call then padded to her bedroom and pulled out a pair of soft cotton lounge pants and a T-shirt as hairs stood on her neck, chill bumps rising along her arms.

She wasn't alone in her bedroom.

EIGHT

The figure emerged from her bathroom, dressed in black like at the Coburn estate and on the roof downtown. Libby's heart rate kicked into high gear, and she spied her weapon on the table by the side of the bed. She lunged for it as the figure sprang with agile force onto her bed, blocking her from retrieving her weapon.

Libby couldn't go on defense. Aggressive. No fear.

She popped the figure right in the kisser, sending him backward on the bed. Her neck throbbed and images of a knife returned to her mind, but she prayed for strength to fight. No more cowering.

As Libby grabbed for the gun, the attacker kicked her in the jaw, knocking her to the floor.

Banging on the front door caught her attention. Axel was back with no way to enter the house, except he knew the garage code and could punch it in.

Her head spun, but she jumped up and went for the gun again as the garage door opened.

Axel!

The black-clad figure leapt through her window; he'd removed the screen and cut through the glass. Libby finally snatched her gun as Axel barreled into the bedroom, weapon in hand.

"He was here." Libby's chin throbbed. Had he broken or fractured it? She pointed to the open window and Axel bounded through, not even asking if she was hurt. And he shouldn't have. His priority had to be The Eye. Not Libby.

She blew through the house, going out the front door, but her street and yard were empty. Daylight had started to dim, but it was still bright enough to see.

She raced down the sidewalk to the west as Axel ran east. Libby weaved and bobbed through houses and streets, asking anyone outside if they'd seen a person dressed in black run by or a car speeding through. But no one had. Where had he gone?

After circling the block, she jogged back to her house. Her neighbor came outside with a petite blonde woman beside him. John had lived beside her for the past three years. A doctor with a nonprofit like Doctors Without Borders. She couldn't remember. He was tall and good-looking. She'd gone out for coffee a time or two with him but had made it clear she wasn't up for a relationship. Guess he'd found one now.

"Hey John. You see a man running by my house? Dressed in all black?"

"No," he said. "Why?"

"My house was broken into. Caught him and gave chase but I lost him." Which begged the question how well did he know this subdivision? Had he stalked it for months, creating routes where he could easily escape without being seen once he decided to strike?

"Whoa. Did you call the police?" the woman asked.

John glanced at her and frowned. "This is a friend of mine. A nurse with my team that travels."

"CeCe Montgomery."

Libby didn't have time for pleasantries. "Hi. Me and my colleague are handling it for now." She blew a breath, her heart still thudding against her chest.

"Oh. The big guy? I see him around sometimes," John said.

She nodded as Axel rushed down the sidewalk, evenly breathing, and met up with them, shaking his head. Libby mimicked him. "This is John Baltzell. Lives next door. He and his friend didn't see anything suspicious."

Axel frowned. "He punch you?"

John's eyes widened. "I did no such thing!"

"Not you." He turned to Libby. "Did he?"

"No. He used his boot."

John's eyes grew wide. "You didn't say you had an altercation."

"And how do you know Libby again? Neighbor?" Axel asked.

"Yeah. I live right there. I saw Libby run by, and she isn't exactly dressed in running gear. Thought I'd come out and see what's what."

Axel studied him. "Why are you sweating?"

John frowned. "I was moving an entertainment center by myself like an idiot."

"I told him I'd help," CeCe offered, and grinned. "He declined."

Axel cocked his head. Libby didn't give him a hard time. Everyone was a suspect, but John Baltzell was not The Eye and he clearly had an alibi in the nurse friend.

"Well, thanks, John." She gave Axel the "cool it" eye. "Keep a lookout for me, will you?" Libby asked.

"Absolutely. Can I take a peek at your chin? I am a doctor." He smirked and without permission lifted her chin, feeling around. She didn't bat his hand away. "Aching and throbbing?"

"Yes."

"Can you wiggle your jaw from side to side without much pain?"

She obeyed without pain.

"Any loose teeth?"

She felt around her teeth with her tongue. "No."

"Probably bruised. Ice it and take some ibuprofen around the clock. If it doesn't improve in four or five days go see a doctor for an X-ray."

"Will do. Thanks." Libby waved, and she and Axel returned inside her house and to her bedroom. "Before you start in, John Baltzell is not our guy. So move along in another direction."

Axel sat on the edge of her bed, surveying her bedroom as a federal agent and not a friend. "Fine."

"I know what that means. You're going to have Archer dig on him."

"He cut the glass on your window like the other victims."

"You're ignoring me." Axel had every intention of looking into John.

"I'm not. I'm thinking about how long he's been stalking you and casing your house and exit routes. He was fast and vanished easily. Which—"

"It's not John."

"Okay." He threw his hands up in surrender, but his eyes said anything but.

Libby stroked her chin, which still throbbed. She needed pain reliever ASAP. "I'm not in the medical field but, what if the reason he targets those women is because it's convenient and comfortable—not because they're in that specific field."

"An easy hunting ground."

"Yeah. He might feel alienated outside of his realm of work. There he feels strong, in charge. Seen as no threat. If he felt powerful outside of those confines, he might very well target women of other jobs—strong women." She snapped her fingers. "Strong women anger him." Libby rushed into the kitchen where the files were strewn on the table.

She flipped from one file to the next. "All of the victims were strong women. Whether they were in charge at their jobs or outside of their jobs. Kickboxing instructor on weekends for the ultrasound tech in Dallas. Receptionist was a surfer in Galveston and had won several awards. Charge nurse. Doctor. The office manager in San Antonio also sat on the board of a nonprofit for a foundation for orphaned children. These are tough women."

Axel looked through the files.

"Cheryl," Libby whispered. "She was a tennis champion and owned her own catering company on the side when she wasn't teaching. She's strong."

"Was," he murmured. "She *was* strong. Physically and mentally."

This vicious killer was definitely playing with

Axel, but he hadn't only chosen Cheryl or Libby because of Axel. He had a twofer—they were both strong women, which made them his type.

Axel's face blanched.

"What's the matter?" she asked.

"Libs, you're the ultimate prize. None of these women, including Cheryl, are as strong as you. That scares me."

"Join the club," she whispered. "I hit him though. He got a taste. Knocked him clear back on the bed and if his legs hadn't been so long, that boot would have never connected and I'd have put a bullet in his brain." And honestly, she wouldn't have been sad about it. Life was precious and this monster had been taking it at his own pleasure for a decade. He would not stop. He was not sorry. He had zero regrets.

"You said long legs. Like he was all legs?"

Libby nodded. "Yeah."

"That's helpful."

"And strong. He works out and is fit. Not your or Bridge's degree of fit, but he works out. He had power behind that kick."

Axel rubbed his chin. "He's been here more than once. He knows you have no camera out back. You need to board it up now." He headed for her garage where she had leftover wood from building a deck last summer. She and Axel had tirelessly worked weekends until it was finished.

After grabbing a few boards and her toolbox, Axel went to work hammering the boards into place. "How do you feel about my ranch?"

"It's nice. Could use a kitchen remodel."

When he turned with a put-out look on his face, she chuckled. She knew what he meant. "I'm fine staying there. I'll pack for a few days, including Dallas tomorrow."

"Good deal."

She went into her closet and grabbed her roller suitcase then began packing while he lingered on the photo of her and Lucas. That was twice now he'd done that. "Why do you keep looking at that photo?"

"You're slimmer in it. I could have pulled that Libby from the ledge a lot easier."

She cackled at his obvious joke-slash-insult. "I was. My boss was less stress-inducing than my present day one. I didn't eat my irritation in cheese sticks so much."

His grin lit up his entire face. "The President and his family gave you less stress than me?"

"Loads less. You're high maintenance." She tossed in two pairs of dressier jeans, a blazer to match all her shirts, and sensible shoes.

"Whatever."

He hadn't answered the question, though. He'd deflected with a joke to start another one of their bits. Did she push it or let it go? Did she want to hear the answer? And was the answer the reason for his deflection? Axel was a lot of things. A liar wasn't one of them. He'd rather dance around a topic than tell the truth.

"You didn't answer my question." Guess she did want honesty.

He pivoted and shoved his hands in his pockets. "I just remember having Cheryl's photos in my bedroom. First thing I saw when I woke and went to sleep. Like she was still there with me. Some nights I put her picture on her pillow. But as time wore on... I moved those photos to the living room and then let them dwindle to one. Not because I didn't want the reminder or because it was too painful, but because I needed to move forward emotionally and I wanted the fond memories not a shrine. Not that having a lot of photos is wrong or bad, just for me, and so... I don't know. I was just thinking that he's still in the most intimate places of your heart."

Her chest fractured a little at that. She'd never slept with Lucas's photo but then she and Lucas hadn't made it to the most intimate parts of a couple's life yet. But having him in her bedroom did feel like keeping him close in her heart. Just because she wasn't going to marry anyone, and Axel wasn't going to marry anyone again didn't mean they weren't moving forward. They were, but he was a little ahead of her. Or...was he?

Why hadn't she taken Lucas to the living room? Was it because she was still keeping him close or was it a reminder of her mistake? Her failure. Her punishment for falling in love with a colleague and making fatal mistakes.

"Is he?" Axel asked. "Have you not moved forward? I don't want to say 'moved on' because we don't ever move on. Life doesn't go on, it morphs into something else. A new normal with a constant hiccup inside to remind us that this isn't the way it was supposed to be. But we can be at peace with how it is now." Axel swallowed hard. "Are you in love with him still? Or are you always going to love him and miss him but you're stepping into a new future?"

Why did he want to know that? What did it matter?

She licked her bottom lip. "I don't know. I miss him and he haunts me at the same time. Of course I love him. I was going to marry him. Spend our lives together. Have children together. Grow old. I just… I don't know."

A pained expression flashed across his face, but he recovered quickly. "I get that. Cheryl's death haunts me. Not so much Cheryl. Anyway," he said, changing his tone to a lighter note. "I'm going to put the tools away."

Libby's phone rang. "Amber."

"Hey."

"Hey," Amber said. "Am I on speaker? It's not work related."

"No." She covered the phone with her hand. "Personal. Not work."

Axel lifted the toolbox and leftover boards. "I'll see myself out."

Once Axel left the room, she closed the door. "What's up?"

"Can't a friend check on a friend?" Amber said in her husky tone. She had the voice of Demi Moore. "How are you? Away from the boys. Be honest. Axel called us earlier when he was looking for the man who attacked you in your own home."

"Axel just boarded up my windows and I was doing okay until he asked me why I still have a photo of Lucas on my chest of drawers, and now I'm a little freaked out." She shared her thoughts about punishment and moving forward.

"Wow. That's heavy. I can relate though. Losing Jack and knowing that he'd gone into that building without calling me in for backup, in order to protect me, made me so angry at him. I remember yelling so many times into the air, 'If you'd have called me you wouldn't be dead!' Once the anger gave way, grief flooded in. Now, I'm numb to be honest. Some days I'm still mad about it. Some days I'm hollow and empty. I try to pray and fill my void with the Word, memorizing scripture about God being our comfort and refuge and hope. But some days the depression swallows me up and it's hard to see any light or feel the warmth of God. I wish I had a pat answer or even help navigating it, but I'm still as lost as a goose two years later."

"I'm so sorry. I know how much you miss that man."

A long sigh escaped through the line. "I'm more interested in why Axel is asking you these questions now. You think he's jealous of Lucas's place in your life? Is something going on with you two?" She wasn't digging for juicy intel; Amber was simply being a good friend.

"No. Well... I don't know. Something has shifted between us. I can't explain it." She confided about what happened in the supply closet. "I don't know why I'm having these big feelings other than the fact my life is in danger and it's bringing up the past and how I felt that night I almost died. And it's got to be bringing up feelings for Axel concerning Cheryl and The Eye. We're crossing emotional wires is all because we are tight. He's my best friend."

Amber was quiet a few moments. "Friends often make the best partners in life. It would be okay for you both if this friendship built on 'we're not falling for anyone so we're safe' nonsense crumbled. But I get not wanting to be vulnerable again. It opens you up to more potential loss and devastation. Y'all's jobs are dangerous. But you can't let fear hold you back from something that might be sensational. Because you don't know that you'd lose him or that he would lose you."

Amber was right, and she'd dated a few times but never found a love match. How did she do it? She didn't let fear rule her world. If only Libby could mimic that, but the fear was too great.

"Working with a loved one causes slipups. Deadly ones. Me and Lucas and Axel and even Cheryl to a degree are proof of that. I love my job and Axel is a cofounder. I don't want to ruin that. And if we did give it a go and it didn't work out, then what? Awkward is the word."

"True. But what if it did? What if you two have felt this way a long time and it's just now coming to the surface because of the danger, and it's not actually projection over the past? Think about it. Pray about it."

Best advice. "I will. I'm doing okay. I'm scared and I hesitated on the roof." She expounded. "But no more. This guy is going down whether or not I'm terrified—which I am."

"We have you covered. Physically and spiritually because we're praying. All of us."

"Thank you." Amber really was the best. "Talk to you later."

"Okay."

The call ended and she slumped on the edge of her bed, staring at the photo of her and Lucas. Were her feelings stemming from loss or from something new she might be realizing with Axel? And if it was the latter, could she ever act on it? Would that be smart for either of them?

At least with a killer she could simply shoot him, beat him.

How would she shoot these feelings down and beat them?

Amber's words about Axel possibly being jealous of Lucas came back, and an idea sparked. She texted their admin assistant, Jolie, for a specific search on CoburnPharma employees. Jolie was efficient and quick and texted back immediately that she was on it.

They might not find The Eye this way...but then again, they just might.

Axel waited in the living room, his mind racing. Why had Libby asked him about that photo? Why hadn't he told her the whole truth? Because she'd made it clear that any feelings crossing a line would be nipped in the bud. He couldn't lose her friendship. So he didn't tell her that part of him wanted her to move that photo to the living room and out of her intimate space, metaphorically. But he didn't know exactly why he wanted that. Why jealousy over a man who had passed ate at the edges of his mind and maybe into his chest.

Libby rolled her large suitcase and carry-on out of the bedroom and her phone dinged with an incoming text.

"You *moving* to Dallas?" he asked.

"If you keep judging my packing, maybe." She smirked, but he noticed something in her eyes he couldn't quite pinpoint. Maybe nerves. Had this attack done her in?

"Hey, things are going to be okay." He laid a hand on hers, squeezing, and she broke free, leaving him to feel a sting of rejection.

"I know." She straightened then checked her phone. "While I was finishing packing, I was thinking about someone who might be after Harley who was pretending to be a loved one—like we've already said. I texted Jolie and had her go through employee files of anyone fired specifically by Harley and to put ones who put up a fight with witnesses around, called HR or even accused him of messing around with their wife or girlfriend at the top of the pile. They might want revenge on him. If Harley had an affair with a married woman once, maybe he's done it before. She just sent me a file. This person could even be The Eye."

Libby scrolled through the text. "Oooh. This man looks like a winner. Hunter Parks. He and

Harley had more than one heated argument over a woman. Several employees went to HR about the arguments and how it made them uncomfortable. That's documented here. According to their accusations, Hunter's girlfriend had a fling with Harley while Hunter was out of town seven years ago. Harley mentioned being bullied as a kid—his sister protecting him. If Hunter humiliated him in front of people in a heated argument, a great way to get back at him would be to sleep with his girlfriend. He lives about fifteen minutes from our office. You up for a chitchat with him?"

Clearly, she didn't want to discuss what was going on, and Axel wouldn't push. Since the supply closet, a barrier had been erected between them. "Who was the girlfriend?"

"Maribel Juarez. She worked for a dentist's office in downtown El Paso."

"Interesting. Yeah. Let's talk to Hunter, and take the pizza with us." Might as well stay busy with someone else's issues instead of his own. He was not a fan of this new tension between them, and he hoped it wouldn't remain this way forever.

Twenty minutes later, they arrived at Hunter Parks's place. Axel knocked on the door. "Who should take the lead here?"

"Me. If Harley had a fling with his girl, he won't trust men and especially not attractive ones."

"You saying I'm good-looking?" He tried teasing, hoping she'd bite.

"I'm saying I should take the lead." Libby's voice was pleasant but distant.

He already missed her and she wasn't even gone, but like a turtle she'd ducked into her shell. Axel could kick himself for the supply closet scene and opening up about that photo on her dresser.

Hunter Parks was a tall slender man, with symmetrical features, thick short hair and warm eyes. "May I help you?"

"Hi. I'm Libby Winters and this is Axel Spears. We're with a protection agency, and I'd love to ask you a few questions concerning Harley Coburn."

His expression hardened. "You're protecting him?"

"No," Libby said. Not a lie. They'd been pulled from detail duties.

Hunter frowned. "Okay," he said hesitantly. "Come in."

They entered his clean and tidy home, which smelled of garlic and lemon polish cleaner. "I just ate dinner. Can I get you a drink? Water? Coffee?"

"No, thank you, but we appreciate it." Libby smiled, and it garnered her one in return. Hunter found her attractive; his pupils had dilated. He had good taste. Libby was beautiful and didn't even know it, which made her even more appealing.

Hunter motioned for them to sit at his kitchen table. Libby sat closest to him. "It came to our attention that you and Harley had some words and he made a move on your girlfriend at the time. Maribel. That speaks to his character, and I'm trying to find a pattern of this behavior." She made sure to lay blame—without actually laying blame—on Harley. She was smooth.

Hunter sighed. "Harley is a jerk. And probably a serial killer. The man has zero remorse. His mother hired me, and we got along great. That was ten years ago. She said I had a way with people and could see me in a corner office on the top floor one day. Harley didn't like that."

"How do you know?"

"Because when she promoted me four years later and gave me an office next to his he became hostile. Dumping loads of work on me and humiliating me in front of coworkers. I'd had enough, and I may have belittled him in front of his staff. Calling him a spoiled, entitled jerk who only had his job because he was a Coburn. Nothing he had was based on his own merit. And that was true."

Libby said Harley had been bullied. He may have seen Hunter Parks as a threat, and his behavior erupted from past trauma. Also, they were only receiving Hunter's side of the story. They hadn't discussed it with Harley yet. But they would. Somewhere in the middle, the truth would surface.

"After the altercation, your girlfriend had an affair with Harley?" Libby asked.

"Not immediately. But Harley Coburn planned his revenge. He wooed and pursued her and seduced her a few months later."

Libby nodded. "Did she recall it like that? Being seduced by him?"

"I don't know how she recalled it. I found them together when I returned home, just like he wanted. I walked out and never spoke to her again. When I returned to work Monday following their fling, he fired me on trumped up charges but he had written me up so he had grounds with HR. But it was all bogus." Hunter all but spit on the kitchen floor.

Something wasn't adding up.

"If it was bogus," Libby asked, "why not fight it? Why allow the write-ups if there was no real merit?"

Exactly what Axel was thinking. Well, at least they were still on the same page investigative-wise.

"Harley is the son of a very powerful family. Who do you think they would have sided with? There was no point in fighting it. Or contesting the write-ups. I left quietly and got a new job where I'm happy."

Libby laid a hand over his, a tactic he'd seen her do before in a move to lower the other person's guard. "That must have been hard. I know I'd want revenge."

"I didn't want revenge. I wanted justice but none came. That's the world. It's unfair and we have to keep treading water." His voice was calmer now, devoid of anger. Nothing left but resignation in his words, but the spark of fire hadn't burned out in his eyes.

Libby stood and Axel stood with her. "Do you think Maribel would agree with what happened? Clearly they didn't stay together. Do you know why?"

"Harley didn't want a relationship. He wanted revenge and got it. And I don't know what Maribel would say. She's dead. Killed herself three days after I found her with Harley in her apartment."

NINE

Axel sat inside the SUV, shocked. And by the looks of it—and lack of conversation—Libby was too. He cranked the engine and put it into Drive. "Is it me or is it odd that she died by suicide three days after she was found in bed with Harley?"

"It's odd, yes." Libby checked her phone. "We can't always know what is going on inside another person's mind."

"I'm going to call Archer. See what he can dig up. He's as fast as Jolie when he wants to be."

He called on speaker and Archer answered, his voice low. "Hey."

Libby frowned. "Why are you being so quiet?"

"I'm...in a room with a lot of books."

Libby snorted. "Why can't you be like a normal man and just say library?"

Archer sighed. "What's going on?"

Axel informed him of their visit with Hunter Parks and how his girlfriend died three days later. Keys on his laptop clacked. "She did indeed die by suicide. Although her family begged the local PD to investigate it as a homicide. They didn't believe she would kill herself, but it appears to be an open and shut case."

Libby frowned. "It's fishy."

"I agree," Axel said. "It wasn't that long ago a killer was staging homicides as suicides. Bridge's brother looked into it, and we found out his eldest sister didn't die by suicide but was murdered, so it happens. It may have nothing to do with anything, but we should look into it based on Hunter Parks's clear hatred toward Harley. What if he hated her too? Enough to kill her and stage it as a suicide."

"Sounds like you need to talk to Harley again. See if he can offer any further information," Archer whispered.

No one ever said Harley was a good guy. He was a privileged, entitled rich boy, and he knew it. But that didn't make him a killer or even a sociopath. "Definitely. We're staying at my ranch tonight. Our flight to Dallas leaves at nine tomorrow morning. It's a one-way ticket. We have no idea how many people we need to talk to. Two so far. Jordan Jenkins and Joel Wickham. Several victims were from the Dallas-Fort Worth area."

"You staying at the Little Ranch?" Archer asked.

He and Axel had several small ranches, some

nonworking, across the state for safe houses. Two had been inherited between the two of their families, and one had gone into foreclosure, which they purchased at a steal. That was the one in the Dallas area where he and Libby would be staying tomorrow night.

"Yeah. We'll keep you updated."

"Sounds good," Archer whispered again.

"Hey Archer?" Libby asked.

"Yeah?"

"Are you checking out James Bond books?" She glanced at Axel and grinned.

"I am James Bond." With that he ended the call.

"Does he ever talk about his time with the CIA?" Libby asked.

"Not often."

"You know Bridge's wife had an assignment with Archer once. Three months they worked together. Yet she never talks about their mission or how bad to the bone he was. He was their top phantom, and I've seen him disguised in front of my own eyes and didn't know it was him. Just makes me wonder what his story is, you know?"

"I do know."

"Yeah, but we don't. I don't. Come on, I won't tell," she teased, knowing she would get nothing out of Axel.

"You're better off not knowing, Libs."

She sighed dramatically as they headed for

Axel's ranch. At least he had security and they'd sleep better tonight. He hoped.

"Call Bridge, will you? Tell him what's going on and we want to talk with Harley on speakerphone. We need him to watch his body cues. Thankful Bridge is good at spotting a liar."

Libby called Bridge as they turned up the long stretch of road leading to Axel's ranch. They passed under the big wooden sign. Axel had yet to name his ranch but the arch was there, with no name. He'd bought it a few weeks after Cheryl died, no longer able to live in the home where The Eye had taken her life.

He'd done a lot of the repairs and remodel himself, keeping his mind off the loss and grief. The place was too big for just him and he'd thought about selling it a few times, moving into a condo or small home. But every time he prayed about selling, he received no peace.

So he stayed and kept a small crew of ranchers to handle the horses and cattle, which made him a good living on top of his protection company but living here alone seemed silly.

He pulled up under the awning instead of the garage as Libby filled in Bridge and Amber.

"Let us get settled, then I'll FaceTime you and you can give Harley the phone. We can all see his face."

Smart. Axel hadn't thought of that.

She ended the call, and Axel opened the back door. "You need both bags or just the carry-on?"

"Just the carry-on. Thanks." Libby hopped out and walked to the door.

Axel used his phone to unlock it. Smart house. Smart locks. Smart security. Inside, he dropped his keys in the bowl on the kitchen counter. "As usual, mi casa is su casa."

Libby had already headed to the fridge and pulled out a sparkling water he kept specifically for her. After taking a swig, she thrust her chin toward his hand, holding his cell. "Let's do this."

"You run point. He responds better to you." Axel made the call and Bridge's face popped up on the screen, his dark beard fuller than normal. "We're ready. Libs is taking point." Axel handed Libby the phone and leaned against the old butcher block countertop.

Harley came into view, his hair mussed on purpose and his straight white teeth gleaming. "Ms. Winters. Are you staying safe?"

"I am. I wanted to talk to you personally. I always feel personal is best."

"I agree," he said with a curt nod.

"We're running a new angle on your case. Possible disgruntled employees who could exploit these women's deaths as a cover to attack you."

His jaw dropped. "That's disgusting. Did you find someone?"

"We think so. Hunter Parks."

At first Harley looked confused, and then it dawned on him and he rolled his eyes. "I don't think so. Hunter and I were never friends, and I had to fire him, but he wouldn't try to kill me."

Libby discreetly explained their conversation, omitting some of the nastier things Hunter had to say about Harley. "Did you know Maribel died by suicide three days later?"

Harley pinched the bridge of his nose. "No. I found out later. I'm not proud of chasing down Hunter's girlfriend, but you can't seduce someone who doesn't want to be seduced. If she was secure and happy with Hunter, she would have refused to have a drink with me, refused dinner on several occasions and when all was said and done, she invited me up to her place. I didn't press or push or ask. But yeah, I started after her on purpose, unsure of what would happen. And to be honest, I ended up liking her. She was a lot of fun and really smart."

"Did you ever think she was suicidal? Did she ever mention depression or turmoil in her life?" Libby asked.

Harley's lips twisted to the side. "Depression? No. Suicidal? No. But she did have turmoil. She wanted a job making more money, and she wanted to end things with Hunter—before I came along. I think she used me a little at first too. I had money and power to help her get a new job, but things changed. This went on behind Hunter's back a solid month. We ended up caring about each other."

Harley was making sense and much of this could be verified. It actually correlated with what Hunter was stating. Maybe she did take her own life.

"Do you believe there might have been foul play?"

"From Hunter?" His grim expression said not a chance. "No. And I don't know of anyone else either. She had no enemies. I was supposed to pick her up for Sunday brunch, but she died Saturday night. I got a call from Hunter. He blamed me for driving her to do that. It was ugly, heated and I hung up on him after saying some unkind words myself. That was that."

She hadn't died like The Eye's victims. But if Hunter was angry enough, he could have killed Maribel and been the one to make attempts on Harley's life, and The Eye was the one after Libby, putting them back to two people instead of one. Hunter *had* called him a serial killer as if trying to make them believe it too, which Axel didn't. He also didn't believe Harley killed Maribel, but he wasn't convinced that she'd died at her own hands.

Finding Maribel's killer wasn't Axel's job, but he would talk to the local PD and the FBI, and if they thought it was relevant to the case they could pursue it.

"Thank you, Harley," Libby said. "I believe you. If you do think of anything else or anyone else who had a vendetta or even an argument with you let us know. Whoever made these attempts didn't necessarily have to be a victim's loved one."

He cocked his head, his eyebrows inching north. "Right. I hadn't thought of that. My biggest concern is that The Eye, who is after you, might also be after me. If people think I'm The Eye, he might not like that and want me out of the picture, permanently. Is that possible?"

"You don't have anything to worry about there," Libby said.

He gave her a pointed look. "I noticed you didn't say yes or no."

"I can't say. I don't fully know. What I do know is you have the best protectors watching your front and back. Don't worry until there's something to worry about. That's what my dad always said, and he was right." Libby's tone was calm and collected and her face a mask of confidence. But Axel knew better than that. She wasn't fully buying her own words, and she personally did have something to worry about.

"Okay," Harley said, but hesitancy laced his words and she saw uncertainty in his eyes. "I'll let you know if I think of anything else."

"Good. Take care." Libby ended the call and turned to Axel. "I have no idea if these are unrelated attempts. But Harley's smart and he's thinking what we've already brought up. The Eye may not like the limelight Harley is getting for his work. This is frustrating."

She wasn't wrong.

"You know what we need?" Axel asked.

"Apple pie with vanilla bean ice cream and caramel drizzle?" Libby's eyes turned hopeful.

"No, well yes, always yes. But I have none of those things and you can't bake to save your life and neither can I," Axel told her.

"Fair. And don't say darts. It's the one stupid game I can't win at."

She was right. Axel could hit the bull's-eye every single time. His record for darts was far better than Libby's. Every now and again she could hit the mark. "True. I love that about you. No, I was thinking, we need to clear our heads. We've got too much information and theories buzzing around in our noggins. Let's go for a sunset ride on Chestnut and François. It'll do us good. Us. Nature. Horses. Fresh spring air. Because temps are already climbing, and it'll be too hot and sticky in a few more weeks."

"I like that idea. Are my riding boots still in the barn?"

"Far as I know. I never moved them."

After changing, they walked out to the barn, the Franklin Mountains surrounding them and the sun slowly dipping, leaving a palette of soft colors and duskiness to the sky. Libby slipped into her riding boots, which she'd left here from the many times they'd ridden before.

Libby had grown up in Texas and wasn't a stranger to horses and stables. She chose François, the bigger horse but a softy. Chestnut could be a little temperamental, but she was Axel's favorite. Guess he liked a feisty female.

They saddled the horses and mounted, then headed out toward the back of the property. A large lake blessed his land adding to the gorgeous scenery. Mosquitos would haunt it soon enough, and it would be misery riding out here. Libby always teased they'd end up with malaria if they rode out here in summer.

"Well, the upside is," she said, "we won't get malaria just yet."

Axel chuckled. "I was just thinking that."

She grinned as they rode off at a steady canter in comfortable silence. Finally Axel spoke. "You really think my kitchen needs an update?"

Libby snorted. "Yes. Your floor is linoleum. At least bring it up to tile. I kinda like your wooden countertops, but you could use some better lighting and updated fixtures."

"I haven't had time, and I'm not in there enough to care I guess."

"You've done a great job on the living space, primary bed and bath and the bath off the living room. You could paint the kitchen a softer color to lighten it up."

"I've thought about that."

"Thinking isn't doing." Libby grinned. "Another dad-ism. But he's right about that too."

Axel had met Libby's family and enjoyed being around Mr. Winters. He was a hoot, and his dad jokes were perfectly corny. Axel's father had passed away some time ago and his mother last year. It was hard not having family. He rarely saw his sister, who lived in Scottsdale. Spears & Bow had become his family.

Libby.

But he wasn't looking at her like a sister. He never had if he was honest with himself. They rode side by side as they came to the lake. A beautiful view. Libby let out a long sigh. This was what she needed. Beauty. Breathing room.

Gunfire erupted, shattering their peace.

TEN

Libby ducked, but she was high on a horse and the shots were too close for comfort.

"Axel, ride. Back to the house." But Axel wasn't listening. Instead, he was moving himself in front of her, blocking the shots. "Axel, are you out of your mind? Just go!"

She turned the reins of François, darting back toward the house at a full gallop. But Axel purposely slowed, staying behind like a red bull's-eye. Her pulse jackhammered.

"You keep going, Libby. I have you."

But no one had him. At the moment, she didn't have time to give him the what for. A sniper was intent on putting one of those bullets into her brain. Whoever was hiding out here had good aim, and any second he was going to hit his target, but the bullet would have to pass through Axel first because he refused to ride beside or ahead of her.

She pushed the horse to go faster, his nostrils

snorting as he made a powerful run to the barn. Another round of gunfire erupted, but she kept going. Definitely a sniper in the distance since no one chased behind them on horseback. It would have been easy to get an ATV out here from the other side of the property. They were at a far enough distance that they wouldn't have heard or seen it from the house or stable, which was now in her sight.

She galloped inside, reining the horse to a stop then swinging off and leading François to his stall and his safety. Once he was secured, she rushed to the stable entrance. Where was Axel? Why had he been so stupid? Reckless.

The first thing she spotted was his shirt covered in blood.

He'd been hit. Again.

Libby's stomach lurched as she attempted to run to him.

"Get inside! I don't know the shooter's location."

She ran back inside the barn. She hadn't heard any further gunfire, but at the moment she was trying not to shoot Axel herself. "You've been hit," Libby roared, furious but terrified. Her hands trembled uncontrollably, and she noticed his hands were soaked in blood too. How bad had he been hit?

Axel led the horse into the stable. "It's a graze.

Looks worse than it is. Not even as bad as the last one." He checked out the wound on his biceps that hadn't been hurt before. "See? You stay put while I do a sweep and make sure you're safe."

Libby didn't have time to protest as Axel left the stable. It felt like days that he was gone, but it was only about fifteen minutes before he returned.

"We're safe—for now," he said, as he returned and slid the door shut, barring it.

No, they weren't. Tears burned Libby's eyes, a mixture of emotions flooding her system. She ran full force at him, knocking him off his feet and to the stable floor with a thud. She raised up and punched his pectoral muscle. "You jerk!" She hit him again, straddling his stomach. "I am not an official client. You should have moved faster, with me, not being my shield. You could have died, you idiot!" She punched him again, this time with force, and Axel let out a raspy grunt and grabbed her wrists.

"Last one I'm taking for free, Libby. I did what needed done to keep you safe." He sat up, forcing her behind to the ground. "I'm not letting anyone hurt you."

"I am not Cheryl. This is not about Cheryl, Axel. Protecting me isn't a second shot at protecting her!" Anger rolled over her in waves for a million reasons. But the greatest seemed to be that she didn't want to be compared to his late wife.

He framed her face. "I do not think you are Cheryl, Libby Jane Winters. I know exactly who you are, and protecting you has nothing to do with redeeming what I lost by failing her." Axel removed his hands from her face and jumped up. Libby stood, trying to slow her heart rate and calm her anger and fear. All that blood had terrified her.

"Is he out there?" Libby murmured.

"I don't think so. He's gone, for now. Not for good, though." His tone was sharp and simmering. He spun on her. "I don't know what you want from me. You want friendship and we have it. Deep friendship. Which means we clearly care about one another so why would I not fight for you, with you? Would you have not done the same for me?"

She would have. Without fail. Without hesitation.

"Lucas—"

He closed the distance between them, clasping her shoulders with his giant hands. *"I'm* not Lucas." He bore his gaze into hers as if willing her to understand something she couldn't, or wouldn't.

"I don't want you to protect me," she said, but the words were strangled with emotion.

"Get over it," he quietly demanded.

"You could die and it would be my fault."

"Libby, if I died protecting you I would have no regrets. Not one." Axel's grip tightened to emphasize his statement.

Her bottom lip quivered. "I would."

"Get over it," he said again, but more gently.

A tear slipped over and streamed down her cheek. "I'm afraid."

"Of dying? Of me dying?" he asked, and inched farther into her personal space, his breath on hers.

Yes and No. Right now, she was afraid of her feelings, and the stirring of wanting something she vowed she would never desire or want again. But it was here now, bubbling to the surface like lava, ready to blow and engulf her whole heart. "No," she squeaked. "And yes, but no."

"Then what are you afraid of? Talk to me," he whispered, his breath ragged and his chest heaving.

She held his inky gaze, took in his dilated pupils.

"I'm about to cross a line," he said breathlessly. His thumb grazed her damp cheek.

He continued to hold her captive with his eyes. Now was the time to tell him they didn't cross lines—that was the whole point of their friendship—but words would not cross her lips.

"Tell me when to stop, Libby. Just say when…"

His lips hovered over hers and her heart thrummed wildly, but still words would not come.

Then Axel's velvety lips flanked in whiskers touched hers, his nose brushing up against hers, rubbing her like a cat's tail around her ankle as he paused, waiting for her to give him one more chance to refrain from what was about to happen, but instead she shook inside with fear, excitement and anticipation.

The word *stop* wouldn't come because she didn't want it to. She wanted this to happen even if she simultaneously didn't want it to happen.

How long had she wanted this? While she'd believed things had shifted between them in a matter of days, her heart told another story, one that had been going on much longer than days.

When she didn't retreat, Axel fully, but tenderly, descended upon her lips, parting them and gently exploring. The heady sensation at his taste, his skill and the emotion backing his kiss, buckled her knees, but he instantly brought his arms around her waist, holding her upright against him without even chuckling at the effect he had on her. There was no arrogance in this kiss.

She tasted the confidence and hope, the devotion and loyalty, and riding under those currents was a stronger, much deeper emotion she refused to acknowledge, but it was there. In the care and tenderness—the purposeful restraint not to let it kindle into a fire they couldn't return from.

Libby fisted the back of his shirt, drawing

him closer as his own embrace tightened. A vise of protection, a refuge for her tender heart and scared soul. She'd never felt more connected, more held, more guarded.

When Axel broke the kiss and ran his thumb along her bottom lip, neither spoke. How could they when they needed air to breathe and to bring their heart rates down?

Finally Axel released a long breath. "I don't regret that."

But she did.

What did this mean? How could they work together now? Why hadn't she had more self-control and said no when she'd had the opportunity?

"You do, though. It's in your eyes." Hurt flashed in his. Hurting him wasn't her intention; she hurt too. How was she to respond? If she admitted she was afraid, he'd counter with telling her not to be. But that was easier said than done. Libby had watched a man she loved bleed out with no way to help him. How could he not see this was going to affect their working relationship? It already had. Axel's bloody shirt was a glaring reminder.

"I don't know what's happening." That was as honest as she could be right now.

Axel let out a small humorous laugh and ran his hand through his hair. "Well, if you don't know then I guess I don't either." He kicked at the hay and entered Chestnut's stall, removing her riding gear and hanging it overhead.

"Are you mad at me?" she asked. That was the last thing she wanted.

"No, Libby. I'm not mad. How about we try to pretend we didn't cross your line, and we never allow it again. Until you figure out what might be happening." He entered François's stall and removed his riding gear, hanging it up as well while Libby leaned against the wall, still tasting Axel on her lips.

How could she pretend that kiss never happened? It was... She had no words for how it made her feel. Or the fact she wanted to march into the stall and do it again. Breath be ignored.

"Sun's down. We can finish talking in the house."

"The kiss?"

He pivoted, his lips pursed. "No, we're not talking about that again, remember? We're pretending it never happened. Easy peasy."

Pulling his gun, Axel inched from the stall and motioned her to follow. She drew her own weapon and they crept back to the house. Axel entered the code to unlock it, and they went inside.

"We have to be up early so you better get some rest. I'll call Archer and the team. Inform them. I can only guess someone banked on us coming to my place—or we were followed. They saw an opportunity when we saddled up and took it. I don't exactly know. Tomorrow we'll be in Dallas and safe."

He started for his bedroom.

"It's *not* easy peasy, Axel."

Turning, he sighed. "No. It's not. Walking away from you is the hardest thing I've done in a long time. But I'm doing it. Because you're right. The pain of losing someone you love is debilitating, and I'm clearly just now at a point where I've moved forward without feeling guilty for it. The ache isn't there quite like it used to be."

That was true. She hadn't thought about Lucas or felt guilt over him when kissing Axel. "Exactly."

He cast her one more forlorn expression and disappeared down the hall to his bedroom, probably to tend to his graze and escape her.

What about the ache she felt now? It was excruciating.

She padded down the other hall to the guest room. Somewhere out there a killer wanted her dead. But all she could think of at this moment was the gaping wound in her heart. It was bleeding out, and she had no idea how to stop it.

Axel stared at the clouds outside the airplane window. He hadn't slept much last night, and when he had, he'd dreamed of that kiss in the stable only to wake to his heart aching for something that could never be. Even if he came to terms with his muddied thoughts about Libby, she was adamant that it wasn't going a toe further.

Did he want it to?

He touched his lips, still feeling Libby's against his. Her words didn't reflect her kiss. Axel had felt more than soft, smooth lips and equally matched energy. He hadn't imagined the hope and hunger. Promise and passion. Friendship and a future. But it had been there grinding against his heart. People of faith didn't kiss like that if there wasn't a future on the horizon. Or at least people like him and Libby didn't. But did he want a future?

She had a point. If that kiss was a glimpse of what they might be feeling, it was deeper than the ocean. Stronger than a Cat 5 hurricane. They were like live wires. If they fell in love and The Eye beat him again and stole Libby from him, it would send Axel to an early grave. Losing Cheryl almost did him in.

They'd been a whirlwind. Dated only six months before marrying and been married three years. It had been beautiful and sacred. He'd meant their vow of till death do them part.

But the thought of loving and losing Libby might literally bury him alive. That was the very reason Axel and Libby found comfort in each other—the boundary lines. Now, neither of them was a safe space for each other.

"What do we know about this Jordan Jenkins?" Libby asked, interrupting his thoughts and drinking a ginger ale. This flight was short but sitting by Libby was distracting, and his thoughts about that epic kiss last night only added fuel to the fire.

Jordan Jenkins was a prime candidate to come after Harley. "His wife was a victim of The Eye, and he also pointed the finger at Harley. Also he works for a rival pharmaceutical company, so there's some tension there."

"And being The Eye? Travel. Medical field."

"Flimsy but yes." They would keep open minds about whether The Eye was presenting as Harley and Libby's attacker or they were dealing with two separate people. Every victim's loved one was also a potential person of interest as the decade-long serial killer too.

The flight attendant brought the trash cart by, and Libby handed over her empty cup. They'd be landing soon. The tension was tight but not unbearable. He hated the weirdness between them, but he'd caused it. He'd crossed the line.

And she hadn't stopped him.

What did that mean? According to her, she didn't know but she regretted it.

But she did know. They both did. The real word was denial. But he'd hold back, and after this case maybe put a little distance between them in order to nip the growing feelings in the bud and let the feelings stirred by that kiss fade.

The plane made its descent and taxied in. After disembarking, they found the rental car agency and rented a newer model Ford Explorer. "We're closer to Jordan Jenkins's home than the ranch and Joel Wickham's, and from Jolie's information Jordan works remotely. Do you want to get food then go to his house or interview and pick up food later?"

"Interview, food, ranch."

Axel entered the address into the GPS and switched on the radio to early '90s pop. Libby's favorite. "I hope this isn't a dead end."

"Me too. But I'm kinda glad we're here and whoever is after me is not."

"I hear that." The threat and the danger remained but for a day or so they had a reprieve. But then nothing was certain, and Axel wouldn't let his guard down simply due to being in a different city.

After a few more turns, the GPS called their destination on the right. Jordan Jenkins lived in a middle class, cookie-cutter suburb. After parking in his drive, they walked up to his house. "I'll run point on this one," Axel said.

Libby nodded and after another round of knocking, the door opened to a nice-looking man with blond hair and dark eyes. Mid-to late thirties.

"Can I help you?" Jordan asked.

Axel identified himself and Libby. "We'd like to ask you a few questions regarding your wife, Annabeth. You mentioned she'd been stalked in the couple of months leading up to her death."

"You're not with the FBI?"

"I actually ran the case until I left the Bureau. I'm now independent." Not a lie but not a direct admission he was working for Harley Coburn, which would be an immediate shutdown from Jordan.

"Oh, yes come in. Please." He welcomed them inside his modest but modern home, and they walked into an open concept plan. "Can I get you a drink?"

"No, thank you," Libby said, and Axel declined too.

"I'm not sure I can tell you any more than I told the police after Annabeth died. She was a nurse in the ICU."

"I'm sorry for your loss," Axel said.

"We were married twelve years. No kids, and I'm glad about that now. They would have been traumatized."

Death was traumatizing no matter the age.

"You said she'd mentioned to you that she'd been stalked or followed?"

He nodded. "She thought someone had been in the house a few weeks prior to her death, and some of her undergarments were missing. She also felt like she'd been followed home from work. I told her to tell the police, but she said it was only a feeling, no proof. Then she was butchered in our bedroom with a hymn stabbed into her. I found her. The police asked me not to reveal that information about the old hymn."

"Did you? Tell anyone?" Axel asked.

His eyes widened and he shook his head. "No. I wanted the monster caught. I wouldn't have done anything to jeopardize the investigation."

"Other than being stalked, did Annabeth mention anything else?"

"One thing. I actually forgot about it in the initial interviews, and I didn't think it was relevant to go back to the cops with. But Annabeth mentioned a guy at the hospital a few days before she died who asked her to lunch off campus, but she didn't go. You don't think it was the killer, do you?"

What if she had gone to lunch and lied to her husband? "It's possible. You say this would have been the week she was murdered?" Axel asked.

"Yes. I believe that's right."

This was potentially useful information and

might aid them. Hospitals had cameras, and sometimes they could be found in the cafeterias. If Annabeth's hospital had caught this on camera, they might be able to identify the man, but that was two years ago and the hospital might not have saved the footage. It was worth a shot to ask, though. "Was this man an employee or visiting? Do you know?"

"She never said."

Wouldn't matter. He could have posed as medical personnel. With big hospitals and many floors, one employee wouldn't know every single person. "So what do you think about Harley Coburn?" Axel asked.

"I think he's a spoiled rich kid who has a job because of his family. But he's good with people, and that sometimes edged me out but not enough for him to be comfortable. He's not a fan of being shown up or beaten." He shrugged. "Rivals will be rivals."

"Do you believe Coburn is The Eye?" Axel asked.

Jordan waved off the notion as a total joke. "At first because I was angry, but no. That would take effort, and Harley didn't do anything that required too much effort on his part. He relied on his charm. Why?" He sat up straighter. "Did he say I'm the one attacking him because I travel from Dallas to El Paso and other places for my job? I assure you I'm not your guy."

Axel weighed Jordan's words. Harley wasn't exactly proactive. He was nonchalant in everything he did even when it came to protective services. This man made valid points. "According to our records, you didn't leave the company, you were let go and at Harley's insistence."

"I'm a better rep than him. He felt threatened. I had a job—a better job—within hours. I don't have hard enough feelings to go after him whether for my wife or personal revenge. He didn't kill Annabeth." He sighed and raked a hand through his hair. "I really don't know what else to say. You're welcome to call my company and see if I've been in El Paso during his attacks. You'll find I haven't."

Axel nodded. They weren't going to get much more, and Jordan Jenkins was probably right. Axel stood and Libby followed suit.

They left Jordan's and swung through a drive-through while Axel updated the team. Archer said he'd call about the hospital footage from the week Annabeth died—if they still had it on file. He'd report back when he knew something.

After talking with Joel Wickham, they knew nothing more than what he'd already stated in the reports but he was still bitterly angry. Maybe too angry to make calculated attacks on Harley, but they weren't ruling him out just yet.

At the small secluded ranch, they carried in

their bags and food. The air smelled stale inside and it was too muggy. He turned the thermostat down, and the air kicked on. Axel set the bags of food on the table and blessed it.

"You think the man *was* Harley that Annabeth ate with?" Libby asked through a mouth full of a chicken wrap with extra ranch.

"If she had, she would have told Jordan that, don't you think?"

"I really hope they have that footage."

Axel ran his fries through ketchup. "We'll find out tomorrow. Then we can talk to friends of hers and other victims' families and hopefully we'll be able to turn our information over to the police." That was the downside to protecting people. They weren't private investigators and needed the local police if their bodyguarding led to a suspicious person.

They ate in mostly silence, making small talk and dancing around the ever-growing elephant in the room. So mature and adultlike. When they'd finished eating, Axel threw away the trash and Archer called. Axel put him on speaker. "Go."

"They have footage, and you're welcome to go over there and look at it. I also called the local PD with the updates, and they'll want to see the footage if you feel it's a lead. They trust your judgment."

"How is it going on Amber and Bridge's end?" Axel asked.

"Harley is business as usual. Working. Playing tennis, acting like nothing is wrong and no threats or attacks since the two of you changed places with Bridge and Amber."

If it was The Eye, that wasn't surprising. He wanted Libby more than Harley.

"He's going to visit his sister later. Also, Amber asked him about office romances based on your suspicion of someone being in the supply closet with him, and he says he's not involved with anyone."

"Then why was he collecting toilet paper when he didn't need it? And for at least ten minutes. I'm almost positive someone else was in there," Libby said.

"I smelled perfume," Axel offered. "Just didn't pay attention to it with so many women in the office."

"I don't know. He's been forthcoming about affairs in the past. No point hiding it now. Maybe he just really likes Charmin," Archer said.

Libby snickered.

"FYI it was the cheap one-ply stuff," Axel said, and Libby snorted.

"I forgot what a toilet paper snob Axel is." Libby sighed. "I'm going to freshen up before we head to the hospital." She rolled her bags into one of the bedrooms.

"She gone?" Archer asked.

"Yeah, why?" Axel took him off speaker and held the phone to his ear.

"Amber mentioned in a passing conversation you two might be moving toward something more romantic. True?" Archer asked cautiously.

"Is that a frowned upon thing? I don't remember us setting that into place when we started this company." Axel hadn't meant to sound that surly.

"I've poked the bear," Archer said, amused. "I'm curious not rebuking or reprimanding. I know I'm behind-the-scenes and you alone know why, but that doesn't mean I'm not involved and in the know. You're my best friend, Axel. You were there for me when...when my world ended and morphed overnight. This thing I'm dealing with now, the secret I have to keep, is the hardest mission I've ever been on and every day I feel like I'm failing."

"You're not failing. You're paranoid and sometimes delusional. Definitely hard to get along with because you're stubborn. Annoying when you're right, which you think is all the time, but you're not a failure."

Archer hooted, exactly what Axel was hoping for. "Tell me how you really feel, man."

"I don't know what is going on with us. Well, yes I do. Nothing. She's made it clear, and the truth is I'm not leading with my head here. My head says to back off. I wish I could rewind but

I can't, bro. We kissed at my ranch, and there's no coming back from that."

"That good huh?" Archer was even more amused.

"It's put a massive wall between us that I'm never going to break down, dismantle or scale. I've lost my best friend."

"I thought I was your best friend."

Axel laughed through a sigh. "It's hard to be your best friend when you keep hiding in the hills of North Carolina."

"You know why I'm here."

"I know. How's that nosy neighbor?"

Archer groaned. "Driving me bonkers."

Axel chuckled. "Oh yeah?"

"Not like she's driving me so far up a wall I want to kiss her. More like I want to put my fingers on her carotid arteries and apply eleven pounds of pressure kind of madness." His tone was frazzled. "All I'd need is ten seconds."

Axel cackled at Archer's description. He'd no more hurt a woman than Axel would, but his spy days were coming out in his humor. Eleven pounds of pressure on both arteries would be lethal.

"I'm kidding. Sort of," Archer said. "I want to make sure you're okay. I can put you on detail with Amber more often if you think that would help. Or you can. You own half this company, but you might not be seeing as clearly as you should."

That was fact. "Maybe. Maybe that's what we need to keep our friendship intact, if we can salvage it. I think I ruined it."

"Nah. It's the Libster we're talking about. She's levelheaded and logical. She doesn't run on emotion, and that's why she's so stinking good at her job. She's like a robot, man. I love it."

Axel knew Archer was simply complimenting Libby, but it caused a hint of green to flow in his veins. "Yeah. Me too."

"Not the same way of course. You know that." Archer's reassuring tone told him he also knew Axel well.

"What do you think I should do?" Axel asked.

"I don't know. You're not putting anyone in danger by loving her, except for yourself. I guess you'll have to see if it's worth sacrificing yourself on the altar of risk and love. But what do I know? I'm hiding in the mountains and trying to keep my head above water."

Axel heard the doorbell. "She back?"

"I'm going to commit homicide. Gotta go." He ended the call.

Well, at least it would be quick. Ten seconds was fast. He chuckled, and Libby reentered the room. "Well?"

"I'm ready when you are."

"I'm ready."

Civil but not overly friendly. Maybe he should assign himself to Amber more often. This was killing him slowly.

ELEVEN

Libby scrolled through the footage from the week before Annabeth Jenkins's murder, her neck tight from the tension. Not just the tension between her and Axel though that was excruciating, but she was setting boundaries. She had to in order to protect their hearts and lives.

Her phone buzzed. Her sister, Cass, checking in. Libby had texted her late last night, needing to talk about her and Axel. Cass had all but said she told her so. She'd tried to warn her that she and Axel had always been attracted to one another and were using not falling in love to spend more time together.

Maybe she was right. Libby had been attracted to Axel. Not when he was married and he'd assisted as an FBI agent on a special task force to find the First Lady's stalker, though she had thought he was attractive, but since he hired her. They had made a real mess.

She quickly texted Cass back that all was well, which it wasn't, and she was going through footage in Dallas and would be home soon. So far they'd seen Annabeth Jenkins with everyone but a blond male. Day after day that week, they came up with nothing.

Finally they caught footage of her in the cafeteria carrying a cup of coffee to a table where a man intercepted her wearing a suit. Blond hair. The angle didn't reveal his face, but his height and build ruled out Harley Coburn. "Can we get another angle?"

The IT guy shook his head. "Sorry."

Libby growled under her breath. "Can you at least zoom in?"

"That's doable." He zoomed in. The man was tall with broad shoulders and filled his suit out nicely, meaning it was expensive and possibly custom-tailored. His hair was short but not buzzed. Trendy. Thick neck.

Annabeth smiled, her face toward the camera.

"She seems on friendly terms," Axel said. "She's smiling and her posture reveals she knows him if only for a short time."

Annabeth laughed and put her hand on his forearm. Nice manicured nails on him. A thick watch on his right wrist.

They carried on a conversation. After about fifteen minutes, they opened their phones. Maybe sharing numbers or some other information. An AirDrop possibly. "Do we know if her phone is in evidence?" Libby asked.

"We can find out." Axel pulled out his phone and texted a detective friend with the PD. A few moments later, he shook his head. "No." Next he called Jordan Jenkins and asked about her phone. It had been two years and Jordan had returned it, the information scrubbed.

Libby frowned. "Looks like Annabeth's lunch date knows where the camera is and is purposely staying out of it."

"I agree. Let's follow him, see where he goes next."

Annabeth turned and waved. The man took a seat at the table, on his phone. Looked like he was texting, but the camera footage didn't pick up the details of the phone screen. Finally after a few more minutes, he stood and circled the opposite direction where the camera only showed his back.

"He knows this facility, Axel."

Like he knew the CoburnPharma facility and Libby's security cam too.

The footage showed him walking toward the front doors, but he kept to the corners and out of the line of camera sight. He was good. The Eye kind of good.

Axel sighed. "You might be right, Libs. This could be The Eye."

Libby's phone ringing woke her from a dead sleep. Her cell phone clock said it was 2:00 a.m. John from next door's name popped up.

"Hello?" Libby asked through a thick, sleep-laden voice.

"Libby this is John..." His voice knocked any grogginess from her, and she sat straight up.

"What is it?" Fear slipped into her veins running her blood cold.

"It's your house. It's on fire. I called 911 and they're on the way. It's bad. You need to come here now."

Here, not home. She had no home. "I'm on my way." She ended the call, jumped out of bed and raced across the hall to Axel's room, bursting in.

"Axel!"

He sprang from the bed, his hair in disarray. "What is it?" Grabbing his gun, he switched on the side lamp. His face was covered in dark scruff, and a crease lined his cheek from his pillowcase, which had bunched.

"My house. My house is burning down right now!"

Axel put the gun on the table and pulled her against him. "We'll get the first flight out."

"Everything I own is in that house. And don't tell me it's just stuff." The photo of her and Lucas was in there.

"I'm not telling you anything except we'll figure it out. Get dressed." He framed her face with his warm strong hands. "Do you know any details?"

"No." Tears slipped over her eyes, and he wiped

them with his thumbs. "But I have my suspicions."

"I do too. I'm just not sure why."

She squeezed his hand, which still remained on her cheek. Just his presence produced a calming effect in her. But she knew her ultimate source of peace came from the Lord, and she was leaning into that as far as she could. Slipping from his room, she returned to hers and packed quickly, washed her face and brushed her teeth, changed and put her pajamas back in her carry-on.

Axel was waiting by the door with his bags, and she caught the scent of mint and his fresh scent deodorant. He rolled her bags out and she climbed in the passenger seat, numb.

Libby gnawed her fingernail. Was this a sign it was time to literally move on like she'd entertained the past twenty-four hours? She and Axel had gone too far, and things were awkward. She feared she might never be able to get that easy camaraderie back, and working together might be too much.

Axel had been reckless twice and been hurt twice. Earlier, when she'd been in her room, she thought of him dying because of her, and the feeling of intense pain had sent her calling an old friend from the Secret Service, Jody Gallagher-Novak. Jody now worked for a crisis management team down in Atlanta. A while back,

Jody had mentioned they were looking for another team member.

They still were.

According to Jody, her boss, Wilder, would be happy to have Libby join the team, but he wanted her to take a week or two and pray about the job switch. What was there to pray about? She couldn't work with Axel anymore. She cared too much about him, about his safety and it would turn into a dumpster fire before it was all said and done. Like her house.

But leaving Spears & Bow would be difficult. They were family to her. But now with literally not having a place to live, maybe this was a sign to move on. Find a new home. In Atlanta.

Her phone beeped, letting her know she had a missed notification of movement on her porch. She must have slept through the initial one. If her house was burning to ash, then the camera was melted by now.

She feared opening it. Dread pooled in her gut. If this was a notification prior to the house burning down, it might be the arsonist—purposefully or not. Either way she didn't think it would be good.

Axel pulled into rental return parking. Libby opened the notification, and her mouth dropped open.

A black-clad figure with a mask underneath stood right in front of the camera, a purposeful close-up. He raised the can of gasoline and then made a sweeping motion across his throat and pointed a knife at the camera.

She'd been right. The Eye had set the fire and been brazen enough to stand there and let her know it. Then he pulled something from his pocket and held it up.

A necklace.

The footage was grainy, but two gold hearts with a diamond in the center hung from the gold chain. Did he think it belonged to her? It didn't.

"What is it?" Axel asked.

"The Eye is responsible, but I'm not sure what this last part means." Panic pumped against her chest and her lungs tightened. Her hands trembled as she handed him the phone and replayed the video.

Axel's jaw hardened and his nostrils flared as he studied the video, and then his face turned white.

"What is it?" Libby asked.

"That's Cheryl's necklace. I gave it to her on our first Valentine's Day together. She wore it all the time even to sleep in. I used to tease her it would choke her or break. But she didn't care." His voice cracked and he watched it again, his hand on his lap tightening into a white knuckled fist. "I looked for it so she could have it on for the funeral, but thought she may have lost it or something. I wondered if he'd taken it."

"I'm so sorry, Axel." She pulled the phone from his hand not wanting him to watch it again. No need to punish himself.

"When we get back to El Paso, you're going to a safe house. It's not up for debate, Libby."

She balked at his overprotective reaction, but she knew it stemmed from seeing this video and a fresh wave of pain and fear from losing Cheryl.

"I know what we said about going on the offense and not being mice to his cat. But I... I changed my mind. It's not worth the risk because regardless of what we agreed to and what we're fighting, Libby, I don't want to do life without you, and he is making a bold statement here. He's going to end you in the way you were almost ended, in the way he ended Cheryl, and my life will be burned to ash because you are my—a big part of my life. And this terrifies me to my very core." His eyes were wide and filled with moisture.

Libby tried to quell the emotions swirling through her. Axel was a huge part of her life too, but he wasn't thinking straight. How long could she go into hiding? No one was actually looking for the real killer. They were pointing at Harley Coburn, and they were getting it wrong. The best way to ease Axel's tension and fear and to keep her safe was to make a move.

A twenty-hour-away move to Atlanta. She would be safe from The Eye who might only be targeting her to mess with Axel, and Axel wouldn't end up dead trying to protect Libby while thinking with emotion and not his brain. But that wasn't the real reason; that was a flimsy excuse. Twenty hours away was more about protecting her heart, and maybe Axel's too.

"He's after me to hurt you most, yes?"

"Yes."

"He won't stop until you're destroyed and I'm dead."

"No."

"Okay."

That was that. Axel would get his way but not the way he wanted. And now was not the time to argue about it. There was no argument to be had. This was her sign.

Even if it hurt leaving. It's what she was going to do to keep them all safe. Heart. Mind. And body.

Once they'd returned the rental and boarded, it wasn't long before they were back in El Paso and in the company SUV on their way to her burned-out husk of a home.

She wasn't sure she was ready to see it. What if it was an ambush?

Axel stood in front of Libby's burned-down home. Bridge and Amber stood beside him while Libby and Cass—her sister—walked the perimeter. Didn't look like anything was salvageable, and Axel watched helplessly as Libby hugged her sister and cried.

He'd seen Libby tear up more in the past few days than in all the years he'd known her. He wanted to be the safe place for her to fall into, but she'd erected a wall and he was forced to respect it.

"What do you know?" Amber asked as she and Bridge walked up, leaving Harley a few feet away in the SUV.

Libby sighed. "Definitely arson. Point of origin was the back of the house. Gasoline was the accelerant but after seeing the video that's a given."

Axel glanced over at the SUV with tinted windows. He couldn't see Harley in the back seat, but he knew he was there, watching. Any day now he'd fire them.

"I've presented the past few days' events and Harley's alibis to the police," Bridge said. "They're officially removing him from the watch list. He's no longer a person of interest, but the news hasn't run with it yet so we're still providing assistance. Even after it circulates, that doesn't mean whoever is making attempts on his life won't keep coming. He received a death threat at his place of business this morning, and the tires were slashed on his car too. I also passed along the information to my sister-in-law with the Texas Rangers. Hopefully, they'll take measures so Mr. Coburn doesn't have to have security around him 24/7. But it's his money, so if paying us makes him feel safe I guess we make him feel safe."

"Libby! Libby!" A male voice drew Axel's attention and her neighbor, the good doctor, John Baltzell jogged to her. She raised her head from Cass's shoulder and wiped her eyes in time for him to wrap his arm around her, nearly pinning her against him.

"Invade her personal space much," Axel muttered.

Bridge smirked. "It's...neighborly."

"She doesn't want his embrace."

"How do you know?" Amber asked.

"I know." He strode across the lawn, littered with debris, soggy from the fire hose water and covered in soot and ash. The air smelled like burned rubber. "Libby," he said.

She turned and quickly escaped John's arms, relief in her eyes. Libby wasn't a hugger by nature, and his abrupt display had stiffened her body and she never hugged him in return. "What is it?"

"We have news. Mr. Baltzell." He dipped his chin in a greeting.

"I told the police I didn't see anyone or hear anything. I smelled smoke and called 911." John stood with his hands on his hips.

"You were the one to call them?" Axel asked.

"Yeah. I stood out here the whole time. I

wanted to go in for fear you were in there," he said to Libby. "I saw your car out front. Scared me."

Axel wondered if The Eye knew she was in Dallas or not. Why notify her with the camera display unless he knew she wasn't inside the house? Otherwise, that would have given her time to escape. Maybe that's what he'd wanted. To catch her when she ran out the door for safety. The Eye wouldn't be able to let her burn. He needed his ritual with the knife. The signature style. But he'd attacked her—and Axel—in a myriad of ways not prone to him. So what game was he playing? None of it made sense.

"If you need a place to stay," John said, "I'm going out of town tomorrow morning and will be gone all week. You're welcome to take up homestead. Fridge is even stocked."

Libby smiled but it was tight. "Thank you, John. I appreciate all you've done and your offer, but I have family in town and I'll stay with them."

Not true. She'd agreed to the safe house, but John didn't need to know that.

"Right. Of course. Well, if you need anything at all, please reach out to me. And maybe even if you don't." His eyes were hopeful, and she was about to shoot him down. Libby didn't do personal relationships and making note he was interested while the air was still hot from the fire was tacky.

"Thank you." Libby avoided the open invitation for more than medical aid or shelter. John nodded and waved at Cass and then put his hand out for Axel to shake. Reluctantly, he did, then John headed back home.

Harley emerged from the SUV, darting his glances around as if someone might open fire on him—and someone might.

"Hi, Ms. Winters. I just wanted to say how sorry I am about your house and to let you know, Mr. Spencer, that I got a text and I need to go back to work for about an hour." His face expressed his apology.

"That's fine, Mr. Coburn, we'll be on our way." Bridge hugged Libby then Amber took a turn. "Call us when the eagle lands and keep us abreast."

Axel nodded and looked at Libby. "You ready?"

"Yeah. I have the basics. But... I can't talk about it right now. Let's go. Cass, call me tomorrow and we'll schedule lunch or something. I'll call Mom and Dad and Brody tonight."

"They still in Florida?" Axel asked as they headed for the SUV.

"Yeah. Cass told them not to come, but my brother might not listen. I'll call him and tell him the truth. He won't tell my parents. They'll all want me to stay with them, but I won't because I don't want to be a burden."

"You're not a burden to your parents or siblings, Libs. But now isn't a good time to go running off, and you agreed to go to a safe house. You could be followed if you don't."

"Doubtful. You said yourself him targeting me is about you. Not really me." She buckled up and closed her eyes. "Running off seems smart."

She had dark half-moons under her eyes and touched her scar. He wanted to fix this. Rebuild her house. Keep her safe. But he had no idea how.

He drove out of the city limits to the small empty ranch they used as a safe house. This was as far as she needed to run. "You need some rest, and tomorrow we'll make a game plan. Squash this. Somehow." Axel frowned and retrieved the luggage, bringing it all inside. The house was a little chilly, but he didn't want to start a fire. "You want me to kick up the heat?"

"As ironic as it sounds, I'd like a fire."

Libby loved crackling fires, romance books she thought no one knew about—but he did—and fuzzy socks. He couldn't help her with the romance books and fuzzy socks.

"Okay," he said softly. "If it upsets you, we'll put it out." He smiled and tipped his head to the side. "I might even find some hot chocolate packets in the kitchen."

Her pained expression undid him, but he forced himself to stand in place and not go to her. She wouldn't want that now that they'd kissed and opened up a can of worms.

"Yeah, that sounds good. I'm going to get settled and clean up. I'll be out soon."

He nodded and went to work making a fire, then he rummaged through the cabinets finding packets of hot chocolate with fake marshmallows. He filled a kettle of water and added the mix to two mugs while it heated. From the kitchen he could hear the water running.

Libby had left her phone on the table, and it buzzed. He glanced at it in case it might be her family, but it wasn't.

The text was from Jody Gallagher-Novak, former Secret Service agent and now security specialist in Atlanta. He didn't mean to be nosy but the preview text was on the lock screen.

Sorry about your house, Libby. Wilder says you can start as early as next week...

He couldn't see the rest of the text, and while he knew her phone passcode and desperately wanted to read the text thread, he refrained from further invading her privacy.

He collapsed in the kitchen chair. Libby was leaving Texas for Atlanta? To work for Covenant Crisis Management? She was...leaving him? That's why she hadn't given him fits about coming here. She was only staying until she left town. Libby believed if she ran to Atlanta, she would be safe and Axel would be too. And that might be true of her; The Eye would never stop toying with Axel. But he actually might go to Atlanta to take a crack at Libby.

When was she going to tell Axel? He'd let it go. See if she'd read the text and divulge she was leaving, walking away. This was his fault for crossing a line even if she hadn't protested. What would his life be like without seeing Libby every day?

He had half a mind to call Wilder Flynn and give him an earful for poaching when Libby was vulnerable, but he knew Wilder. He would never poach anyone. He was a man of faith, honorable and trustworthy. If he was allowing Libby to come work for him, then she'd made her decision very clear and gave good reasons. Still, he wanted to punch something. Kick something.

The tea kettle whistled, and he turned it down on low to keep the water hot for when Libby returned to the kitchen. He went into the living room and poked at the fire and wood, listening to it crackle, watching the sparks fly and inhaling wood smoke.

Libby entered the room with her hair down, wearing sweats and a Cowboys T-shirt. Man, he'd never seen her look so good. And he'd only seen her hair down once before. Now all he could imagine was that kiss and her taste. "Water's ready. Just pour it in."

"Okay," she murmured. "Thanks." She padded into the kitchen, and he heard her stirring a spoon in her mug. "Axel, you want?"

"No."

"You put mix in your mug, though."

"Can't a person change their mind?" he snapped, instantly regretting his surly tone and mood.

Libby didn't say anything, but she didn't return right away. When she did enter the living room, she had her phone in one hand and the hot chocolate in the other. She sat beside him on the couch, and he stood. He couldn't sit here by the fire with her and pretend nothing was transpiring between them. Couldn't sit here and not want to kiss her again, touch her hair, hold her close to him and make her feel safe or ask her about that text. Nope.

"Where are you going?" she asked.

"Bed."

The day had been long between flights, seeing the house and dealing with insurance and then updates at the office on the case. It was a little past dinner now, but he was exhausted emotionally more than physically.

"Would you sit with me awhile?" she asked, and the tenderness nearly broke him.

"No," he said softly. "You can't have it both ways. That's not fair to me. I'm drowning over here. Okay? So I'm going to bed." He didn't give her a chance to respond. He went into his bedroom and quietly closed the door and crumpled on the bed, praying God would take these feelings away from him. He was inept and afraid to care for her, but he wanted to care for and protect her. Only she was moving on as far as Atlanta. Running from whatever this was between them. Running for running's sake and using a killer as her pathetic reason.

Even as he prayed, he felt no peace. And if Libby left him, he might never recover.

Axel didn't need The Eye to torture him. Libby was doing a great job all on her own.

TWELVE

Libby sat by the fire and reread the text Jody had sent her. Had Axel seen it? He would never enter her phone, betraying trust, but if he saw the text preview he would know she was leaving. Is that why he was irritable?

Sorry about your house, Libby. Wilder says you can start as early as next week, but things are emotional for you and he wants you to be absolutely sure. We're also working on our end to help discover who might be The Eye. All hands on deck! If you need anything let me know. I feel so bad and we're all praying for you and your team to be safe and put this nightmare to bed.

Was she absolutely sure? No. But she'd been second-guessing herself since Lucas died. This was as much to protect them physically as their hearts. Axel wouldn't see it was the smartest move to make. She'd been praying, but her emotions were so jumbled she had no clue if she was hearing from God or not. She just kept taking all these hits as signs to go, but sometimes hard circumstances couldn't be outrun. At times you had to stay, stick it out and trust God. So which was this?

The fire was dying down, and she'd long drank her hot chocolate. She was exhausted. In a complete brain fog. It was beyond late, but she couldn't find rest. Axel hadn't come out of his room. He'd been right, though. Libby couldn't have it both ways. She couldn't lean into his warmth and strength, taking from him only to push him away at other times. She'd set the boundary, and it wasn't fair to toy with either of their hearts. But the only person she wanted for solace was Axel.

And this was why she had to leave.

She pulled the blanket on the back of the couch over her and rolled onto her side, letting tears come as she begged the Lord to speak so loudly she would have no confusion at all, but she didn't hear anything except…what was that?

Libby sat up and listened. Was that a child? It sounded like baby cries. What on earth? Was it an animal near the ranch? She went to the back door where it was coming from and peered out but didn't see anything. The cries grew louder.

She opened the door and stepped out into the chilly night.

A force knocked into her, dragging her to the ground. She used her elbow to thrust into the masked face, which resulted in a man's grunt. He grabbed her by the hair and ripped her backward, rolling her onto her back. She looked up into that plastic mask underneath the ski mask, but it wasn't the face—or lack of it—that terrified her. It was the large glinting knife in his hand.

"This is going to be fun. Like a cat leaving a dead little sparrow on the doorstep for the owner." His voice was low and raspy and unrecognizable.

She froze. The thought of another blade plunging into her flesh. Axel waking to find her butchered and dead like Cheryl. No. She would fight.

"Not today," she panted. But the man had her legs pinned by sitting on them and one hand wrapped around her throat making her unable to scream for Axel. She could bite, but he was fitted in leather and it wouldn't end in a release from her throat. He touched her cheek with the blade, and she felt the pinch and sting of breaking skin. A drop of warm blood trickled down her face, dripping onto her neck.

She swung with her free hand, but she missed him by a half an inch.

"Not so strong now, are you, Libby? Where's all that power that kept you hanging on a roof's ledge? You're nothing. You're a weak, pathetic woman who thinks she's powerful and tough. Look at you. Breathing heavy with fear and panic in your eyes. You make me sick, little sparrow. They all make me sick. Nothing but little songbirds pretending to be eagles. But my eye has been on you." He hurled a few insults and ran the blade along the side of her trunk, lifting her shirt minimally and sliding the blade along her belly.

Another pinch and sting resulted.

He'd cut her again. Shallow. Toying with her like a meaningless plaything. She swallowed hard. She was not weak or pathetic. She calmed her breath as two more stings broke along her ribs. He was enjoying this. This is how it went with all his victims. Shallow cuts that eventually turned into a frenzy of deeper slashes until they bled out, his god-complex holding their lives in his hands. He determined when they'd die and then he'd leave the hymn stabbed into their chests—an anthem that he was their god, watching. But the only one singing because they were happy was The Eye when they died.

She couldn't reach his face, but she might be able to… Using her free hand, she swung again, this time connecting to his gut with enough force to knock some breath from him and cause him to release his grip. Rising, she butted him in the head and shoved him backward, using all her might, which was a lot when she put all her muscle into it.

The knife skittered to the ground, and she called out for Axel. She tackled the masked man, and they both went for the blade as she called out for Axel again and again.

The Eye grabbed the blade first and rolled over and slashed her cheek, shocking her. Noise sounded inside and he glanced toward the door then back at Libby. "We're not done yet, little sparrow. My eye is still on you." He bolted into the night as Axel made it to the back porch. He fired at the figure running into the darkness and started to run but paused.

"Go, Axel. You can catch him, shoot him!"

"No. You're a bloody mess, Libs." He fired one more shot into the darkness.

"Axel, end this! Go."

"You're bleeding all over. I'm not leaving you, Libs! That's it!" he said with force then knelt, lifting her shirt to inspect her wounds. He winced at the many cuts. "Superficial." He then removed her hand from her cheek, and his eyes instantly filled with moisture. "Oh hon. I can't give those stitches. We have to go to the hospital. We've been compromised here anyway."

"Are you sure?" But she knew the wound was deep. Knew it would scar her for life like the one across her throat. She wasn't being vain or shallow, but another scar for her to have to stare at each day was too much to bear.

"I'm sure."

"Why didn't you go after him?" she insisted. Axel could have gained ground and put him down with a bullet. Ended this. She wasn't going to bleed out. "He's going to come back."

"You are more important, and I didn't know how bad the cuts were. I stand by my decision."

This was why she didn't want them to love each other. He chose her over chasing after the suspect. He'd made the wrong choice.

The same choice she would have made if it had been Axel sitting here.

Libby had needed six stitches to close the wound, and the plastic surgeon had done it to keep the scarring minimal, but she would carry a faint one for life as she suspected.

She wanted to cry but held it in.

The PD had shown up to take her statement and the team had been briefed, but she'd made it clear she didn't want them here making a fuss; she couldn't handle it.

Hours later, they finally arrived back at Axel's ranch. They'd been compromised. How this time? Axel swept for bugs and found none. That didn't mean one hadn't been placed somewhere they hadn't wanded.

She didn't want to go to Axel's, but she had no choice. This was too much to handle. Too much to bear. Why would God keep allowing so much pain to be dumped on her before she could even catch her breath from the last nightmare? It hadn't even been twenty-four hours since her house had been burned down and she'd lost everything.

She'd taken a pain reliever and was now on the couch. She and Axel hadn't talked about what had happened, but he'd been standing beside her when she gave her statement to the police about the child cries luring her outside and seen his jaw tighten and twitch indicating his irritation.

It was a rookie move. Criminals often used baby cries to bring women outside to investigate only to be ambushed. The CSI team had found the recorder, but they didn't find any prints. She wasn't surprised.

"Why?" Axel asked as he entered the living room. "Why would you go outside over a baby cry? We were in the middle of nowhere, Libby. Why would a baby be out there?"

Good questions. She was angry with herself for the blunder. "I've been repeatedly attacked in less than a week. My house just burned down, and my life is upside down so forgive me for being in an exhausted brain fog and thinking it might be an animal. *You* should have chased after him, but I was more important than catching him. And that is *your* mistake because you could have ended it tonight. But don't worry. I'm ending it myself."

Axel scowled. "What does that mean?"

She stood, her heart pounding and aching at the same time. "It means I love you."

His face looked as startled as she felt saying it.

"What?" he whispered, and took a step toward her but she held up her hand to halt him. If he came any closer, she'd lose her courage.

"I love you, Axel. I didn't mean for it to happen." Her voice cracked, and tears burned the backs of her eyes. "And that's why I let you kiss me. I wanted it. But your actions tonight are the reason I don't want to love you. I made a rookie mistake, but you let a killer go for me. It could have ended tonight. No more scars." She touched her face. "No more fear. But your love for me hindered you. You're in love with me." Saying it out loud, knowing it could never be, hit her so hard she lost her breath and couldn't control her lip trembling. He loved her. Why did he have to go and do that? Why did she?

A sheen glazed his eyes. "I do," he murmured. "I am. I'm in love with you, Libs."

She held her hand up again and squeezed her eyes closed, hoping to hold back the dam of tears that wanted to erupt, then opened them. "I don't want to love you, Axel. And I don't want you to love me or something worse will happen. Look at me. I'm a walking pincushion for killers!" Her voice cracked, and he ignored her demand to stay at arm's length.

Instead, he pulled her against his chest, where she felt his heart beating as wildly as hers. "You are beautiful. Scars and all." His hand lightly lifted her chin. "All I see is bravery and strength. And I *do* want to love you. I'm sorry for not giving chase. Neither of us can be sure it would have ended." But his face revealed the truth. He could have had him tonight.

She pushed away. "Yes, we can. So I'm ending this. I'm leaving for Atlanta. I've taken a job with Covenant Crisis Management. We can work without fearing for the other's safety. In time, our feelings will fade. Distance will help it move faster."

"No, you're wrong. If that was the case, it wouldn't be love, it would be infatuation. I am not infatuated with you, Libby. This isn't about some itch to be scratched. Please don't leave. Let's work it out. We can do it." The pleading in this big, strong man's voice shattered her in pieces, but this was best. It was.

She wiped her eyes. "I don't want to. And I'm done discussing it." Because she felt like she might die if she had to keep looking into those gorgeous black eyes that revealed how crushed he was. And she'd done it. She'd hurt him. Hurt herself.

To protect them.

This wasn't about her job as much as it was her heart. His heart. If he couldn't be strong enough to do it, she would. She'd rather break him emotionally than watch him die before her eyes.

He cradled the sides of her head in his hands. "I'm not Lucas."

"No, but you made a Lucas move. Three times now. What happens the next time? I will not watch you die. I can't. I'd rather never be with you and know you're alive than watch that." She inhaled deeply and removed his hands. "I'm going to bed. I'll let Archer know myself. I have to settle things tomorrow with the insurance company, but I'll leave the day after. Jody said I can stay with her until I find a place and get on my feet. It's a good company, and I'll be in good hands."

"I don't want you in anybody's hands but mine, Libby!" he roared, and she flinched. "I'm sorry. I didn't mean to yell. But you're deciding everything and leaving me out of all of it. I have no say. That's not fair or right."

"I agree. And yet this is the way it is. The way it has to be." She spun on her heel and headed down the hall knowing Axel wouldn't follow. Wouldn't press or push. It wasn't his way.

She thought she'd feel peace after making her decision.

But once again, she felt nothing but pain.

THIRTEEN

Axel stewed inside his office, spinning in his office chair replaying last night. He had half a mind to pick up the phone and demand Wilder Flynn rescind the offer to Libby, but Wilder wasn't a man you told what to do and Axel wasn't *that* guy.

Libby had confessed her love, and those words had rocked his world but then before even processing it, she'd shredded him and tied his hands in the matter.

Libby didn't want to love him. She believed time, with distance, would fix it. Axel disagreed to some extent. A week or two apart wouldn't make him feel any differently. He supposed feelings ebbed when one side didn't reciprocate. In time, he would be able to move forward once again, but he didn't think he'd ever not love Libby Winters. He would attempt it though.

She'd given him no choice, which begged the question, did she actually love him? Could someone who truly loved another person—even when that person had harmed or betrayed them—be able to walk away? He didn't think so.

Axel never intended to fall in love with Libby. And yet here he was, miserable.

But the fact that maybe Libby didn't really love him if she could let him easily go would help him tread water.

Amber entered his office. "Hey boss, there's a man here to see you. He says his friend needs some help and wouldn't speak to anyone except you. This is twice today. First Libby with that lady who wouldn't see anyone but her, and now you. What are me and Bridge? Chopped liver?"

Axel's stomach knotted. Didn't feel like coincidence. "Do I know him?"

"I don't think so. He's older and not exactly a crayon box full but he's adamant, and I figured you could use the distraction. You've been in here for hours." Amber's smile softened. "I'm going to miss her too. Not the same, I know, but we're all sad."

Amber had no idea. Or maybe she did. Libby might have confided in her. "Where is she?"

"In her office."

"Where's Coburn?"

"Break room while we do paperwork. He said it was fine with him." She shrugged.

"Send that man in. The elderly man, not Coburn."

She saluted.

A few moments later a man in his early to mid-seventies entered. Thinning hair on top. Bright blue eyes behind wire-rimmed glasses and he dressed like Mister Rogers. "Can I help you, Mr....?"

"Charles. Mickey Charles," he said in a wobbly tone.

"Come sit."

The man toddled inside and slowly eased into the chair.

"What can I do for you, Mr. Charles?"

"I have a friend in trouble. I believe The Eye serial killer might be targeting him."

That got Axel's attention and he sat up, leaning forward on his desk. "What makes you say that?"

"Because he's been acting like a fool. Letting that killer keep him bound up in his house afraid."

Axel gave a gentle smile. This man was mistaken and confused. "Sir, you tell your friend that he's safe and likely not a target of The Eye. He's caused a lot of panic and fear. But staying in his house and not coming out isn't healthy." The Eye didn't target men, except apparently Axel. "Would you like me to call this friend? Put him at ease." He'd heard of blonde women dying their hair brunette when a serial killer was targeting college age girls with blond hair. This guy was becoming an agoraphobic.

"I do believe that's good advice." The man grabbed his forehead and squeezed, removing latex until a shock of dark hair popped out. "You should take it."

Archer!

The man had been the CIA's top phantom, blending in so well family wouldn't even be able to tell. He'd fooled some of the team not too long ago and here he was fooling Axel.

"You jerk," Axel teased as Archer ripped the rest of the latex from his face and donned his signature black, square retro frames. "Why aren't you…? Where…?"

"Taken care of. I needed to be here. At least for an hour or two to tell you what a dope you and Libby are. She turned in her notice before dawn this morning. She was honest with me about why she's leaving, and before you get huffy with Wilder Flynn, he made it clear he would not allow her on the team until she was at peace and sure."

"She might be sure, but I doubt she has any peace. I don't. But I can't deny she's somewhat right. I could have ended it. I could have put a bullet in him, and I chose her. I was too afraid to leave her, I think."

"Because that killer has you locked into fear believing he can take anyone you love at any moment. He's not sovereign, Axel. And neither are you. You won't come out of your own shell. Living in what ifs and paranoia. I know what it feels like to not lose one person you love but all of them. In one fell swoop."

"And you live on the back side of a desert. Metaphorically."

"Not out of fear or paranoia. Out of necessity, and you know our situations are completely different." He gave Axel a dark stern eye.

Archer was right. Fear had been holding Axel back from falling in love, but his heart ignored the fear and went right on and did it anyway. "Well, tell it to Libby."

Archer grinned. "I did. An hour ago when I came in as a tired mom of four."

Axel snorted. It was Archer who'd asked to only speak to Libby. "What did she say?"

"She called me a jerk and a bad mom." Archer laughed and Axel joined in. That would be something Libby would have said. "But she's been living in a cocoon too."

"Did she take your advice to heart?"

Archer pulled a face. "No. She's leaving tomorrow. Anything that needs wrapping up on one of her clients, she's handling today. But sometimes it takes a while to make the words sink in and then stick. I told her she could always come home no matter what."

Home.

She didn't want a home.

"Maybe this is for the best as much as I've been telling myself it's not. If she really loved me, she wouldn't leave, and certainly not with an excuse that doesn't hold water, so maybe she only thinks she does."

Archer stood. "If you believe that, then you're even dumber than I first thought. But you can't force her into anything and begging and pleading will only make her mad. Nor is it your style."

"True."

"We need to look at files for new hires or try and sweet talk Wendy Spencer into foregoing full-time motherhood to work with us."

"Never happen."

"I know. But we have to find a new team member. Two on two. Works best that way." He left the room and heard Amber holler.

"Archer! That was you? Oh Mylanta, was that you as the mom earlier too? I hate you." She laughed, and then Axel heard Bridge chime in.

"You look better as a woman."

Axel chuckled but his heart ached. Libby was leaving. For real.

"How long are you here for?" Bridge asked.

"An hour then I have to get back."

"Back where?" Amber asked.

"Where I came from." Archer loved the mystery and giving his team fits. If they knew the truth, no one would be laughing.

After an hour of paperwork and skipping lunch, Axel knocked on Libby's office door.

"Come in."

Axel poked his head in the door. "Hey."

"Hey."

"You getting everything cleared out and ready to go?" He tried to keep his tone even, but it was hard to do.

"Yeah. And it's not like I have a lot to pack. I pretty much have what's in my luggage and on my back."

"You eat lunch?"

"No. Unless half a pack of Mentos counts." She smirked.

"You want to grab a bite? I haven't eaten either." Should he mention Archer's stunt? She hadn't. He'd follow her cues.

"Um...no. I'll just grab a pack of crackers out of the vending machine. I'd like to get everything done. My flight leaves tomorrow at 6:45 a.m. I'm leaving my car here for the time being. Just some prelim stuff for now. Then I'll come back for my car and finish up anything left with insurance on my house."

She didn't want to spend time with him. "Can

I at least take you to the airport? Before you say no, we're friends, Libby. That will never change. I'll always be here when you need me. I want to talk to you at least once a…month." She'd have denied him weekly conversation, but he was wilting inside.

Libby opened her mouth to say something then closed it and gently smiled. "Okay. I'll be at Cass's. Before you start in with I'm not safe, Bridge will be outside on duty. Amber will be on watch with Harley. She can handle it, and it's not like we never go solo. I was going to have Bridge take me to the airport. I need to be there by 4:30 a.m."

At least someone was seeing to her safety that she'd allow. "I'll be at Cass's around four. That good?"

"Yeah. Thanks for offering…friend." She tried to crack a smile, but it didn't reach her eyes.

How was he going to do this? How would he let Libby Winters walk away?

Libby sat at Cass's dining room table with a cup of lukewarm chamomile tea. Cass had the night shift so she was alone with her thoughts. She was really doing this. Leaving. She hadn't wanted to agree to Axel taking her to the airport in the morning, but she did want to be friends with him. And in time they might be able to get back what they had before things skated over the line. Deep down she wasn't fooling herself. They could never return to the friendship they once had; it had led to falling in love.

She'd allowed Archer's words to echo in her mind. He'd shown up like a frazzled mom of four kids and disguised his voice so well she'd believed a real mom had come looking for their services. The man was frightening with how well he could disguise himself.

He wasn't wrong in his counsel either.

Libby was afraid. She had every reason to be, and she was doing everything humanly possible to keep her and Axel safe physically and emotionally. And therein maybe lay the issue. Human strength could only take them so far. But God didn't prevent the debacle with her and Lucas. She'd lived and Lucas hadn't. Why? Didn't God give them brains to use to help themselves? That's what she was doing. Using her brain to keep them safe. To throw this killer off her scent. Axel let him go and put her first. He wasn't thinking about catching a bad guy.

He'd made Libby his first priority, and it was those kinds of thoughts and actions that got people killed.

She carried the cup to the kitchen and dumped the rest of it. The evening had been a whirlwind of phone calls and tying up loose ends before her early flight. Libby headed for the couch to try and wind down and keep her racing thoughts at bay. She turned on a favorite sitcom she'd seen dozens of times as background noise and to try and divert her thoughts away from Axel and his strong arms. How could arms like granite feel as gentle and warm as velvet? So much for redirecting her thoughts.

Libby's phone rang. Cass was calling. She noticed the time was almost 2:00 a.m. She must have fallen asleep. She woke quickly and answered. "You coming home early?"

"Ms. Winters, this is Detective Swan from the El Paso PD. I'm at the hospital with your sister, Cassandra. She was leaving work early and was jumped in the parking lot. You were her emergency contact in her phone."

Libby's mind swirled. Cass must have been leaving early to surprise her and take her to the airport. Her sister knew how hard it was going to be riding with Axel and having to say goodbye. Someone jumped her? "Is she…?"

"She's alive, but pretty roughed up."

"I'll be right there. Do you know any details? Is she talking?" Libby asked as she jumped off the couch and scrambled to find her shoes, purse and keys.

"She's not right now. She was found unconscious, but it appears to be personal. Nothing was stolen from her, and the car hasn't been jacked." Detective Swan's voice held compassion, and she appreciated that.

Oh Cass. Her heart sped up and she locked the door behind her as she made her way down to the stairwell.

"No one at her place of employment saw anything. We'll get to the bottom of it. Rest assured."

"Thank you." She raced outside and Bridge jumped from the car.

"What's happened?"

"My sister's been hurt at work. I'm going to the hospital, and I may not be able to go to Atlanta depending on the issues so just go relieve Amber and I'll call and update you when I can."

"Are you sure, Libby?"

"I'll be on the interstate and then in a public hospital. If it makes you feel better, I'll call you before I leave and you can tail me or something."

Bridge smiled. "That does make me feel better. But following you and seeing you get inside safely makes me feel even better. Praying she's okay."

Libby agreed and hopped in her car and peeled out of the parking lot, arriving in record time and waving to Bridge. She sprinted inside and headed for the ER. They redirected her to a room. Inside Cass lay on a crisp white sheet, but her face was swollen and black and blue.

This was why she didn't say much. She couldn't. The attack hadn't been done with hands but some kind of weapon. A bat. Tire iron maybe. Libby's heart shattered and she crumpled, kneeling at her sister's bedside. "Oh Cass. I'm here, sis. I'm here and it's going to be okay."

Who would have hurt her sister? Why? If it wasn't a robbery, then what had possessed a person to do this to her?

Cass moaned and Libby perked up, taking her hand. "It's me, Cass. Can you hear me?"

"Yes," Cass said through a strained voice. Her eyes were almost swollen shut, but she slowly turned her head in the direction of Libby's voice.

"Do you know who did this to you? You see them?"

Cass's nod was almost invisible.

"You knew them?"

"No. Saw… Spare." Cass moaned.

Spare? "What do you mean, Cass? What is spare?" she asked.

Cass must be reliving the brutality as her face pinched and she moaned again.

"Hey, it's okay. Rest. Just rest."

"Hi," a voice said, and entered the room with another rolling bed. The nurse was petite and blonde with wide blue eyes. She looked familiar, but Libby was so flustered about Cass she couldn't place her.

"Hi. I'm Libby, Cass's sister. What can you tell me? I'm on her HIPPA forms."

"She's a tough lady. She suffered some internal bruising and she's fractured her arm, but the fact nothing else is broken is unexplainable." She bebopped next to her, fidgeting with the monitor.

"You look familiar."

The nurse smiled. "I get that a lot."

That's when Libby noticed she wasn't wearing a badge. She glanced over at the gurney and frowned, and then the familiarity crystalized.

As she spun around, a tiny pinch in her neck made her flinch and the room suddenly began to spin.

"Easy, Libby. You don't have long before you'll be out completely."

Libby's faculties were fuzzy, but she was aware she was being led to the gurney and eased down onto it and covered with the standard white knit blanket. The nurse laid her hand on her brow. "You've been my man's object of affection way longer than a woman should, so I'm going to put you out of his mind myself."

Libby's last thoughts were of Axel.

FOURTEEN

Axel's stomach had been in knots for hours. He couldn't sleep. He was putting Libby on a plane to Atlanta to secure a new job.

But the truth was if she stayed, they couldn't go back to what they had been. They'd crossed that line in the stable. And he wasn't a beggar. He wasn't going to drop on his knees and plead with her to give them a shot. However, he was tempted but that would only fuel her fire to walk away, and she wouldn't find it endearing but pathetic.

Instead of sleeping, once he knew it was useless, he'd gone inside his room he'd used to work on The Eye case.

He had to be someone who could travel to many locations around Texas. Travel nurse. Pharmaceutical rep or even a doctor who spoke at conferences. Although they weren't limited to those careers.

Libby had no medical training, but she was a strong woman and she was connected to Axel, which had put her in the spotlight. The Eye had been hunting her for over a month and even been inside her home. The longer he drew out the game, the more pain he extracted from Axel.

This was about them now. Maybe it had been for a while. Two tough guys as opponents. But he never physically came for Axel so he wasn't a fighter per se, but he was quick and agile. Athletic didn't mean able to go into combat. Axel was trained. So he used his wits and Axel couldn't deny the man was smart. Always a step ahead.

What bothered Axel was the fact they couldn't find who was attacking and threatening Harley Coburn. A regular Joe would have made mistakes, left prints and maybe even wanted to be caught. Wanted to be seen as a vigilante of justice. But there had been no prints on any of Harley's death threats or the one left on their SUV at the motel. And that made him—as well as Archer—believe whoever was attacking Harley was also The Eye. He was angry that Harley was receiving his glory, and that's why he took the opportunity to attack Libby at the Coburn estate. He'd been there watching.

Why couldn't he crack who the killer was? He sat at his laptop and pulled up Jordan Jenkins, whose wife had died at the hands of The Eye. Next he would look more closely at Joel Wickham. At this point he was hoping simply reviewing possible suspects would reveal something new. His hope was thin, though.

He did an in-depth search on him.

Jordan Jenkins had been married for twelve years. His mom had a tragic, fatal accident falling down the stairs when he was sixteen, and his dad remarried a year later putting Jordan into a blended family with one stepsister. Katy Dribbs.

Axel continued digging in deep areas only a trained officer would know or a really big true crime junkie. He also had access to information the public didn't due to his job and his and Archer's credentials.

Jordan was often in trouble at school. He'd been sent away to a summer camp for troubled teens when he was fifteen. Petty theft, disobedience, violence at school. None of that would raise a red flag. Rebellious teenagers often did stupid things and regretted it as adults. However, now that this new information was coming to light, this was an absolute red flag.

He was sent to juvenile detention for aggravated assault on his stepsister. He was clearly violent. Axel suspected Jordan's mom's fall wasn't an accident at all. Possibly payback for sending him to a troubled teen camp, which Axel turned his nose up at. He had never been a fan of those kinds of places.

Jordan Jenkins's father had passed away of an

illness a year ago, but Axel would like to talk to Katy or even the stepmother, though according to his search they'd been divorced prior to his illness. He searched Katy Dribbs. It was the middle of the night, but this was beyond important. If he could find The Eye, Libby might rethink her Atlanta offer.

He found Katy's number and called, praying she would answer. On the fifth ring a groggy voice said, "Hello?"

"Katy Dribbs? My name is Axel Spears. I'm a former FBI agent who worked The Eye serial killer case, and I own a private protection firm now. I apologize for waking you at this hour, but time is of the essence and I'd like to ask you a few questions regarding your stepbrother, Jordan Jenkins."

He heard shuffling on the line as if she were crawling out of bed and turning on a lamp maybe. "I don't have any contact with Jordan. I don't even consider him my brother. He's a monster, but he hides it well beneath the charm and charisma. If you believe he's that awful serial killer, then he probably is. He knocked me off our roof when I was thirteen and said it was an accident, but my mom didn't believe him. She ended up divorcing his father because she realized quickly Jordan was trouble. She even suspected he'd pushed his own mother down those stairs."

Axel didn't doubt her.

"What about his wife?"

"Annabeth was my dearest friend and when Jordan turned on the charm, I begged her not to fall for it. It ended up with our friendship severed—he turned her against me. After college I moved as far away from Jordan as I could and lost touch. I heard Annabeth died by that serial killer, but I can't say I didn't wonder if Jordan mimicked the killing or was the actual killer."

"He had an alibi, but I'll be looking even more closely now." Jordan could have manipulated the system somehow. Sent his credit card with someone else and told them to use it. Anything was possible.

"He's vile, and I wouldn't believe a word out of his mouth."

Jordan had told them about a guy at the hospital, and a guy had been there that day, but it wasn't Harley—that much had been clear even if the actual face hadn't been.

Axel's blood turned cold.

Annabeth had known and been comfortable with the man. What if the man was in fact Jordan Jenkins himself and he was The Eye—playing games with them even now and sending them on a wild-goose chase looking for someone else and casting suspicion on Harley Coburn in a subtle way?

"Thank you. Talking to you has been invaluable."

"Please don't tell him you talked to me. I wouldn't put it past him to come here and harm me or my family." Her voice held fear, and he understood revenge.

"I won't say a word." He thanked her again and ended the call as he headed out the door to pick up Libby.

He pulled up at Cass's apartment building and went straight inside and to the door. No answer. Libby could sleep soundly if she was exhausted. Had she overslept? He called her phone, but it went to voicemail. He knocked again.

Nothing.

He tried Cass's phone in case Libby had changed her mind about the ride to the airport. She might text him last minute to say goodbye, taking the coward's way out, or not even say goodbye at all. Cass's phone also went to voicemail.

Axel's heart lurched into his throat, and he used his tracking app to detect Libby's location but her red dot wasn't moving. It wasn't even on the screen. She'd turned it off.

Well, that made sense. She wouldn't need it anymore since she was no longer on the Spears & Bow team. But something felt wrong. Axel retrieved a lock picking kit he kept on him at all times from his suit pocket and used it to enter Cass's apartment. The TV was on and the volume low, and Libby's luggage still sat at the foot of her bed.

She hadn't left town.

Where was she? Nerves went off on full alert through his body. He tried her phone again and when it went to voicemail, he texted for her to call him ASAP then he called Bridge. He hadn't seen his car out front, but it went to voicemail. He then called Archer as a cold chill swept through him.

He answered on the first ring. Of course, he would be up before roosters crowed. "Did Libby delete her location app or did you scrub it when she resigned?"

"Neither. I had hopes she'd come back from her preliminary visit and change her mind. Why?"

Dread settled in his gut. "We have a problem." He explained everything, including his call to Katy Dribbs earlier. "I'm going to call Dallas PD and have them check on Jordan Jenkins. Call it a welfare check. I have friends there. He travels for his job, which means he could be in El Paso right now."

Archer's sigh filtered through the line. "Let's be rational here. Do call. But don't panic. We'll find her, and there could be a logical explanation for this or Bridge not answering his phone."

"Archer, your calm-down tactic isn't working

on me. He has her." The Eye would do to her what he had done to Cheryl and so many other women. He'd already threatened it on camera and sliced her body and face. Axel's heart was dangerously close to having an attack. What if he didn't find her in time? Where would The Eye take her?

"Libby is trained for these kinds of circumstances. She just needs one good punch and she'll knock him out. She can hurt him. The woman is smart and savvy."

"I know Archer but..."

"You love her. I know. We all know and have for a long time. We pray and we work smart. We do not panic or do anything rash."

No, he wouldn't. That's what got Lucas killed, and going berserk wouldn't help him think methodically but he couldn't deny he was in a state of frenzy. After he ended the call with Archer, he called the Dallas PD; they were sending a unit to Jordan's house. Best they could do and that was as a favor to him and Archer.

Axel couldn't stand around and wiggle his fingers. He had to find her. He called Cass's work, and an employee gave him horrifying news.

Cass had been brutally beaten last night/early this morning and taken to the hospital. While he was concerned about her, his heart slowed as it dawned that Libby was at the hospital and Bridge most likely with her.

But if she hadn't scrubbed her app, why was her location not turned on?

Axel wasn't taking any chances and he rushed to his SUV, making it to the hospital in record time. Rushing inside Cass's room, he found her broken and bruised.

Shock poured over him. This had been a brutal beating, and she was hardly recognizable. Cass would likely have no idea if Libby had come by or not. They clearly had her medicated to help with pain management.

Why hadn't Libby called a single team member about this? Axel understood her not calling him, but why not call anyone else?

His phone rang. It was Amber.

"Hey, do you know where Libby is?" He didn't have time for pleasantries. "I'm at the hospital. Cass was beaten to a pulp, and I figured Libby would be here but she's not and her location is off. I can't track her."

"That's awful, Axel. I'm so sorry but I have more bad news. We ordered dinner late last night and after we ate, we passed out. And I don't mean like a nice long nap after a Thanksgiving meal. I think The Eye intercepted our food before it made it to the door and drugged our drinks to knock us out. Bridge woke me when he arrived literally five minutes ago when he came to relieve me."

That explained why his phone had gone to voicemail. He was taking care of Amber and Axel had been so worried over where Libby was, he hadn't actually checked Bridge's location dot.

The Eye had made his move. He had Libby. Axel felt it to his bones. "Are you all okay?"

"I'm fine but feel hungover."

But not Harley? Had The Eye come for the man who had inadvertently stolen his thunder? Axel thought he might wretch. "Harley?"

"He's been taken, Axel."

Libby woke, groggy with her vision blurred and her hands and feet bound. The last thing she remembered was recognizing the nurse and then a pinprick along her neck. She'd been drugged. How had she gotten Libby out of the hospital without anyone knowing?

With no idea what time it was, she wondered if Axel had figured out she was missing yet. She glanced around at her setting. Libby was inside a home, in a room dimly lit, and she lay on a bed. As her eyes cleared, she gasped.

She was in Axel's room and this was his bed. What was going on? Why would that woman bring her to Axel's ranch, and how had she gotten them inside?

Libby inhaled and noticed the smell was all wrong for Axel's home. This was his bedroom, but it smelled stale and musty with a hint of mothballs. Definitely not Axel's scents.

The bedding was his and the paint—she'd helped him pick out the color and do the work. A photo of him and Cheryl sat on the dresser... that was *not* right. Axel only had one wedding photo on his mantel.

This was not Axel's home.

Chill bumps rose on her skin and she used her core to get into a sitting position, surveying her surroundings and already working out her exit strategy.

Putting the extra plastic from the zip ties in her mouth, she pulled, tightening them even further until they nearly cut off her circulation, then she brought her arms up over her head, elbows out and took a few deep breaths before slamming her hands down and breaking them apart.

She swung her legs off the bed and got to her feet. If she could find something to help her break the locking mechanism on the zip ties at her feet, she would have a fighting chance, although all she really needed was free arms and an opportunity for an upper cut to the chin.

The drawers to the nightstand were empty. She tried the dresser. Empty.

She hopped into the bathroom and spotted a toilet paper holder. After removing it, she broke it and pulled out the spring. She slipped the sharp end of the coil into the locking mechanism and her zip ties popped open.

Now to get out of this place.

As she hurried to the bedroom door, she heard a man and woman arguing, but their words were muffled and she didn't want to stick around to eavesdrop.

Libby raced to the window, sliding back the curtains.

The window had been boarded up. She rushed to the other window and found the same situation.

Libby bit back a frustrating cry and realized her escape wasn't going to be easy. She would have to fight them both. Going back inside the bathroom, she snatched the metal spring from inside the toilet paper holder and straightened it further until it was long enough to stab someone. She had no other weapon, and this would poke out an eye or rip a throat if she used it right.

"Don't tell me what to do!" the woman screeched, and Libby heard footfalls coming toward the door. She quickly kicked the zip ties under the bed and jumped on it, shoving her feet under the blanket at the end of the bed and holding her hands together between her legs to appear bound.

"I see you're up."

Macy Davis, the admin assistant who'd overheard them talking in Harley Coburn's office, stood before her, her blue eyes wild with madness. She'd pretended to be a nurse and sneaked her out of the hospital.

She swept her hand out. "What do you think? Looks just like Axel's room, doesn't it? It took a while to get it just right, but we did. We have such big plans for him. But you...well, I'm over you. I thought burning your house down would give me a chance to take you, but your stupid neighbor is like a watchdog and I didn't need to be seen."

"Joke's on you. I wasn't home."

Macy scowled. "Yeah, I found that out later."

"Were you on the roof?" She thought it had been a man. No, it had.

"No. I just gave him access." She grinned. "I did leave the note on the car at the motel, and took a few shots at you two while on your romantic horseback ride, and did a bang-up job on Cass. I needed a way to get to you. Found it!" she said brightly.

Anger surged but Libby forced herself to remain calm. Macy Davis would pay for her part in all of this, especially for what she'd done to Cass.

"Macy, I told you not to go in there!" a voice boomed.

The door opened and The Eye stood in the doorway.

Libby looked right into the eyes of Hunter Parks—one of the men who had worked for Harley and been fired. Harley had seduced his girlfriend, Maribel, and she'd died three days later by suicide. But the team and her own family believed foul play might be at hand.

Looked like Hunter and Macy had struck up a Bonnie and Clyde relationship to frame Harley. Macy might have been Maribel's killer and Hunter's alibis in the cities he hadn't actually been in when The Eye had struck. Macy could be Hunter's partner in crime. If so, why hadn't she used her own signature, even a slight deviation from the way Hunter killed his victims?

Libby could only guess that Macy's killing was simply to be with Hunter out of a warped sense of love and devotion. She wouldn't need her own signature. Following his to an art would be her way of showing utter devotion and adoration.

But she had gone off on her own to threaten Libby and burn her house down in a jealous rage. She clearly didn't like the attention—the drawn-out cat and mouse game—Hunter had been giving Libby.

"We got this little ranch at a steal. I've been living here, but things are going to change when you're out of the way. He's been obsessed with you, with Axel. It's what's been keeping him from making us a forever package. But with you and Axel gone, I'll be his object of affection again. Won't I?" Macy turned to grin at Hunter.

Hunter's eyes blazed with fury. "This is going to cost you, Macy."

Macy showed no fear. "I can take some punishment, hon."

"This is all wrong. It wasn't supposed to go down like this!" Hunter threw his hands in the air. Would he kill Macy for messing with his perfect plan? What was the perfect plan?

"She dies in this room today or tomorrow. Doesn't matter. She dies like Cheryl."

"But Axel isn't here to see it this time!" He punched his fist into his other hand. "Don't be stupid. I need to figure out what to do next. To fix this." He stormed from the room, slamming the door behind him.

"He just needs to get Axel here and that won't be hard." She held up Libby's watch. Macy must have been eavesdropping on the team talking in the conference room about the Locale App that was a measure of safety for them. She switched on the app on the watch. "Won't be long now. You think I didn't know he was taking you to the airport this morning? I got that out of Cass. He's running scared. We've had eyes on you the whole time and been so smart and sneaky. You never saw us coming."

Libby grinned and Macy's eyes widened. "What?" she demanded.

"You switching that GPS tracker on isn't going

to have Axel running scared. He'll be coming in like a whirlwind, leaving fatality in his wake. But you won't get to see it."

"And why's that?"

Libby sprung from the bed and coldcocked her, knocking her clean to the floor. She didn't have much time. She undid Macy's belt and hauled her onto the bed, binding her hands together and to the bedpost. She found a taser in Macy's back pocket and snatched that, keeping the spring in her pocket if she needed it for anything else.

After removing one of Macy's socks, she shoved it inside her mouth to keep her gagged, then she hit the 911 button on the watch. Macy wouldn't know about that app or how to trigger it, so the team would know Libby was alive—for now. She quickly put on the watch.

Now to find Hunter Parks.

The tables were turned and *her* eye was now on him.

As long as she didn't freeze again.

FIFTEEN

Libby cracked open the door from the bedroom into the living area of the small ranch home. If she had her way, she would be long gone before Axel and the team arrived. She didn't want him walking into a re-created bedroom to relive the death of his late wife. What kind of sick monster was Hunter?

The empty living room held sparse furniture, but Macy had told the truth—she'd been living here. Libby searched the room looking for something she could use as a weapon besides her toilet paper spring, and taser. She gripped the taser and kept to the walls in case Hunter returned. What did he think Macy was in the bedroom doing? She was clearly unhinged and unreliable due to her warped jealousy issues. Wasn't he worried she'd continue to screw up their plans?

Libby peered outside the living room window, which wasn't boarded. The sun had risen, but it was still dusky at nearly 6:00 a.m. She checked her watch to figure out her location. She was about fifty miles south of their El Paso office.

No texts from the team letting her know they had received her 911 alarm. They wouldn't want to tip off the killers if they snatched Libby's watch from her again.

The GPS would bring them.

Quickly, she texted from the watch.

I am safe. Have my watch back. Hunter Parks is The Eye and Macy Davis, Harley's admin assistant, is his accomplice. They're together.

She hurt Cass. Took me from hospital. I'm getting out of here now.

They'd keep tracking her, and she took comfort in that. Once she crept to the front door, she turned the knob to freedom.

But freedom didn't come. The door was locked from the outside; Hunter and Macy had made this ranch a prison.

However, not all the windows had been boarded. She started for the living room window, prepared to bust it open if she had to when she heard movement from the hall on the other side of the kitchen. She dove behind the couch, taser in hand and ready to pounce if needed.

Hunter mumbled under his breath. He was furious things weren't going his way. As he headed for the primary bedroom where she had been kept, she crawled around the couch to keep hidden. Time was about to be up for her when he saw Macy bound and Libby freed.

She jumped up and darted toward the way he came in. Through a garage maybe. As she raced down the hall, she heard a noise and a grunt. Pausing, she peeped into the crack of another bedroom and gaped. Harley Coburn was bound in zip ties on the bed.

If he'd been taken, was Amber okay? Fear raced through her blood. She couldn't leave him. She slipped inside and his eyes grew wide.

"Libby!"

She motioned for him to be quiet. "Are you okay?"

He nodded and whispered, "They drugged us and took me last night. It's Hunter Parks and Macy Davis."

"Is Amber alive?"

"I don't know. All I remember was eating my meal and waking up here."

Libby prayed Amber was alive. Her hands trembled and she retrieved the toilet paper spring.

"What is that?" he asked.

"A makeshift weapon. Hold still." She inserted it in the locking mechanism of the zip tie binding Harley's hands, and it released. Then she did the same for his feet. "We have to go. Now."

"Libby, little sparrow, come out come out wherever you are," Hunter singsonged.

Libby glanced toward the door. "We need to go through the window. If we enter the hall, we're sitting ducks. Actually, you go through the window and just run as far as you can. I'll take care of Hunter Parks."

Harley's eyes widened. "What are you going to do?"

"Whatever needs to be done." Libby hurried to the window and peered out. They were secluded, but she imagined another ranch would be along the road at some point. "Get somewhere safe. Or hide in the pasture. You have your watch with tracking. We'll find you."

"I don't feel very manly leaving you here."

Libby smirked. "No offense, Mr. Coburn, but you're a noose around my neck. Having you gone and safe means I can focus on what needs to be done here." She slid the window open. "Out you go."

He hesitated until he heard Hunter closer than he had been before, calling for Libby as if it was a game. Hunter had to know she was in here with the client she'd been paid to keep safe even if her duties had changed and she'd been taken off personal protection.

Harley scrambled through the window. "Come with me. We can run together. Don't play the hero, Libby."

He had a point but if Hunter caught them or had a gun, they'd both be dead. She had a duty to protect her client. Hunter wanted her most. Harley was more of an annoyance to kill than a tasty bird to bite into. A sparrow the cat desired. "I'll be along shortly. Go." She closed the window as Hunter's footsteps grew closer.

He was at the door. No escape. She rushed into the closet and held the taser in hand. When he opened it, he'd be in for a surprise. She'd at least knock him down long enough to bind him or wound him with the shank she'd fashioned. Libby would only take a life if it was self-defense.

She hurriedly sent a text to the team.

I freed Harley. He's on the run. I'm behind him.

The door squawked open and Hunter entered, his feet shuffling along the carpet. "What did you do with him?" Hunter murmured, and paused at the louver doors to the closet, which hadn't been shut completely and he'd noticed.

"Make me think you went out the window when you didn't. Nice." He jerked open the doors and Libby lunged, shoving the taser into his side and hitting it at full force. It knocked him to the ground, seizing. He had maybe thirty seconds before his physical capabilities returned. Libby had nothing to subdue him with and the team was on its way.

She climbed out the window and bolted. She had two options. Pastureland that stretched for miles but with little cover or the road. Libby chose the road, hoping she'd happen upon the team on their way. As she ran around the front, she spied Hunter's car and raced toward it to check for the keys.

Bingo!

She jumped inside and started the ignition. Half a tank of gas. They couldn't be that far from a town. She peeled out of the drive of the little ranch and fishtailed as she headed for the road, hunting for Harley as she drove.

About a quarter of a mile ahead, Harley leapt from a deep ditch onto the side of the road, waving her down. She hit the brakes and he bounded inside. "How'd you get the car?"

"He left the keys inside."

"Dumb for him, good for us." He grinned.

"Agreed. Now let's get out of here. Do you have a cell phone on you?"

He shook his head.

"Can you work the navigation system? Put in our address." She rattled it off. "I recognize the Franklin Mountains." She had their location on her phone, but it wouldn't cast to the car's system.

Harley messed with the touch screen entering in the Spears & Bow offices. "What exactly is going on? Are Hunter and Macy dead? How long have they been an item? I have so many questions."

"Hunter and Macy are working together and a couple. Probably hooked up while he still worked for your company, and they kept it a secret so they couldn't be linked by anyone and when one was killing miles away the other had an alibi. Because the way they killed is identical with no subtle changes, it made sense to believe it was one killer. I never suspected a woman as the second killer."

Harley blew out a breath. "How would Macy have the physical strength to plunge a butcher knife that deep and that many times into a woman? It would take a lot of force or rage to do that. If it's a duo, Libby, I think it's two men, not a man and woman. Sounds like you have it all right minus the gender of the partner. Or... maybe there is a woman and she's one of their lovers. Doesn't do the actual killing for them but it's possible she helps them in other ways."

Chill bumps rose on her skin. She hadn't thought of three of them. But that would mean... She slowly reached for the taser.

But it wasn't in the console anymore.

She glanced over and a wicked grin spread across Harley Coburn's face as he held it up. "Hi, little sparrow."

Axel raced down the back roads, following the GPS. Relief had flooded him when he'd seen the 911 come across the app and then the text.

Hunter Parks and Macy Davis.

He could see Hunter Parks but Macy? She wouldn't have the strength needed to do the damage The Eye did to his victims. Bone had been nicked, meaning it had taken a lot of power to go through layers of skin and muscle and tendon to get to bone. But when adrenaline was running on high, women had raised cars off children. Anything was possible.

The smell in the supply closet came to mind as he glanced at the GPS, working to fit the players in place. He was within two miles of Libby, and Bridge and Amber wouldn't be that far behind him.

His phone rang and he answered on Blue Tooth. "Talk to me, Arch."

"You're headed for a ranch recently purchased by a Macy Davis unless Libby is on the run. Local PD are headed to the ranch now. Twenty minutes out, maybe twenty-five. Bridge and Amber have it too, and they're about fifteen minutes behind you." His tone was calm and cool as it always was. "I wish I was closer. Could be there."

"I know why you can't. It's okay. Libby's handling herself as we all know she can. But I'll feel better once I have her in my arms."

"Yeah?"

"Now is not the time for jokes."

"It's always time for jokes. Lifts the pressure

some. But the truth is, I'm worried she's walked into an ambush. Macy Davis as a subordinate? I'm not buying it."

Neither did Axel and his gut wrenched. "Neither am I. And Hunter Parks doesn't give off those vibes either."

"I ran a check on him last night and he had solid alibis for some of the murders but not all of them, not the ones that Harley Coburn had alibis for. Are you thinking what I'm thinking?"

The killer had been under their noses this entire time.

"Harley Coburn."

"I think we don't have a duo at all," Archer said. "I think we have a triangle, and Harley is pulling the strings. He did this to have an alibi for the attacks on you and Libby. To have a front row seat in this sick game. A game he created."

Axel was afraid of that. "Macy isn't in a romantic relationship with Hunter Parks. She's in one with Harley Coburn, knowing full well he's The Eye. She was in that supply closet. It was her movement and perfume. She must have hidden behind that old copy machine when we opened the closet door. Harley had slipped in there to be with her or confer and when we went in, he used toilet paper as an excuse. They had to keep their relationship a secret to keep their wicked deeds hidden too."

Axel hit the steering wheel, angry that his wife's killer had been in plain sight. In his car, in Libby's home. He wanted to vomit. "She easily could have eavesdropped on us while we talked in the other conference room, hearing our plans. She could have laid the GPS tracker on our vehicle while Libby gave chase at Harley's estate. But he and Hunter are the killers."

"Hunter may have killed his own girlfriend to prove something to Harley unless she really did kill herself, but I don't suspect she did. I think he did it out of some kind of loyalty to Harley. Maybe they set that whole firing and fling story up to make sure no one would suspect they were partners. I'm so sorry I didn't see it and you had to be in his presence. They pulled this off seamlessly if we're right, and I believe we are."

Axel didn't blame Archer. He hadn't seen it either. "I blame myself. I was looking at Jordan Jenkins, and I still say he's a sociopath but he's not The Eye or an accomplice."

"We underestimated Harley. Didn't see a triangle coming. And I know what you're thinking."

"I doubt that." Axel was going to rip Harley Coburn limb from limb when he got ahold of him.

"Vengeance belongs to God, Axel. Last I checked, you weren't Him."

Okay, maybe Archer did. "I know. I feel like

such a fool—Harley's fool. I don't think anyone tried to threaten or attack him. I think he used Hunter or Macy or both to pretend to shoot him so he could hire us. Be right there the whole time laughing in my face!" And they fell right into the game. No more games. He was done playing.

"They're going to pay, Axel. We know who they are, and they will be found and dealt with to the utmost extent of the law."

"Hey, there's a ranch up ahead. I'm going in."

"You might be one on three, Axel, if Libby's... unable to help."

Injured. Dead. The thought sent a new wave of terror through him. "Not a problem." He had skill and fury on his side. At this moment he could push a mountain into the sea.

About a quarter of a mile ahead, he pulled to the side of the road. He grabbed his rifle from the trunk, two tear gas bombs as well as extra ammo. His side piece and ankle weapon were in place, and a knife hung off his belt. He was ready to go in guns blazing.

He wasn't going to lose Libby.

When this was over, he was going to knock some sense into her heart. For now, he was ready to knock some heads. End this. For good.

On foot, Axel made his way to the ranch. He

used his sniper rifle scope to search the perimeter. Two cars.

He texted the team.

On site. Not waiting. Going in.

Waiting could get Libby killed. He noticed the side windows had boards on them. That must be where he was keeping her. If she was inside. Last text said she'd freed Harley. But she didn't realize he was The Eye.

If she caught up to him...tried to protect him...

Axel's stomach roiled and knotted as he approached the house with caution, peeping through the windows in the back of the house. He knew he was walking into a trap. Why else would they turn on the tracker? They had purposely meant for Axel to breach the ranch as part of their plan.

But Libby had retrieved the watch. And what was the plan to be exact?

"I wouldn't if I were you." Hunter Parks spoke from behind Axel. "Someone wants to see you."

Axel slipped his hand in his pocket and clutched the tear gas grenade. "Fine."

"Drop the rifle."

Axel obeyed.

"Turn around."

"You got it." In one quick movement, Axel pivoted and pulled the pin on the tear gas grenade, tossing it at Hunter. Gas erupted and Hunter shrieked. Axel snatched up his rifle. Hunter would be blinded for fifteen to thirty minutes. Bridge and Amber would find him aimlessly wandering and unable to see. But just in case, he pulled his gun and fired, wounding him in the leg and dropping him to the ground. He wasn't going anywhere now.

Anyone inside the house would now know for sure that Axel had arrived.

But he didn't care. He entered the silent building, clearing the mudroom, living and kitchen area and moved to the room with the boarded windows.

He paused upon entrance. This was a complete remake of his own bedroom. Had Coburn taken photos after killing Cheryl? The thought nauseated him. Beside the bed, Macy Davis was bound, with a bullet through her forehead. Libby wouldn't have killed someone in cold blood who was incapacitated. Looked like Hunter or Harley had done it.

Now Axel was down to two men.

And he wanted Coburn.

"You like it?" Harley said from behind Axel. Axel slowly turned. Libby was bound, hands behind her back, feet tied with rope and her mouth duct-taped. Harley held a knife to her throat. "I could go right over the scar. But I'd like to give her a new one. Although with my cut, there won't be any healing. No scar. Pity." He drew Libby even closer. "Women like you make me sick. Like my own sister. Trying to bully me and stand up for me, making things even worse. I hated her. She was my first attempt at ending a life. It didn't end in death but now she's like a harmless little kid. I've been getting it right for a while now. I'll make sure you don't live through the pain—long."

"Let her go. This is about us." Axel stepped closer to Harley.

"That's far enough." He pressed the knife into her throat and drew blood. Libby screamed beneath the duct tape, and her helpless, fearful cry enraged Axel.

"You're going to regret that."

"I doubt it." Harley looked at Macy. "Women. They're too emotional. She ruined my well-thought-out agenda. She'd become a liability anyway. We gotta let them go when it's time, don't we? Burning down the house, beating up Libby's poor sister. Not my agenda or timing."

Axel remained silent.

"Man, you have no idea how thrilling it's been to be right under your nose. In your house—again—in Libby's—again and neither of you idiots having any idea."

Axel was already calculating Harley's moves. He'd want him to drop his weapons. But he and

Libby could take him by hand. No problem. He had to remove the knife from Harley's grasp first.

"Here's how this is going to work. You lay all your weapons down. Tie yourself with those cords, and then you'll get to watch the show. I'm going to do to Libby what I did to Cheryl. Man, she begged. I do love it when they beg." Harley chuckled and Axel's hackles rose.

Libby's eyes held a calm Axel needed and she slowly shook her head, reminding him to be smart. Harley was pushing all the right buttons to throw Axel off his game and rile him up. Enrage him. Enraged men made mistakes. Frightened men became reckless.

Axel would keep his cool. No matter what.

He dropped his rifle and side piece as well as the ankle piece.

"A real John Wick, aren't you?" Harley shoved Libby forward another step. "Tie your feet."

Libby's biggest fear holding her back from him was that two people who worked together and loved each other would take reckless risks. Axel was going to show her that wasn't always the case. He could save her and be levelheaded at the same time.

But he would have to take a calculated risk based on skill. If he bound himself, it was over. What he needed to do was the only thing that would save them both.

"I still have another item to drop," Axel said and looked at Libby, revealing with his eyes his intentions. This was the reward of a deep, abiding friendship and love. Conversations without words.

Libby frowned then her eyes widened as she understood and barely nodded, revealing she trusted him with her life, and that said everything to him. Axel hadn't said weapon, he'd said item, i.e., Harley. "You ever play darts, Harley?"

"What?" He sneered. "Shut up, Spears. We're done talking."

"You're right about that."

Harley pressed the knife into Libby's neck, blood instantly pooling.

"Mistake," Axel said, seething.

Libby let her body go limp like deadweight, buckling to the floor, giving Axel the half of a second he needed to draw his blade and throw it.

His knife landed on the mark, instantly dropping Harley to the floor. Dead.

Axel scrambled to the floor, removing Libby's duct tape. No finessing it. Libby winced and rubbed her mouth and fell against him. He retrieved his pocketknife and cut her feet and wrists free. Her arms encircled his neck.

A car sounded in the drive. Bridge and Amber.

"It's okay now. I have you." He held her tight against him, hoping it wouldn't be for the last time.

"All I could think is you'd come in guns blazing and get us all killed," Libby said.

"Well, one of us has more confidence in the other person. Thanks." He chuckled and kissed the top of her head. "I told you we could work together. We wouldn't make mistakes." He lightly tipped her chin to look at him. "I love you, Libby Winters. I don't want you to move. I don't want you to quit. We make a good team."

"What if I hadn't ducked?" She grinned.

"I had an inch of space. I wouldn't have missed."

"I believe you. I did have confidence in you—in the end."

He chuckled.

"And I love you. I did say it first, you know. I've been terrified because of the past. It's been dictating my future, forcing me to draw a line I didn't really want to draw, Axel. I want a future. With you."

A massive weight lifted from Axel's chest. "That's music to my ears." He held her hands and noticed red marks. Not from the rope. "You got free before Harley found you. They have you in zip ties?"

"Yeah." She removed a coiled spring from her back pocket about six inches long. The end had been pulled into a sharp point. "I MacGyvered it. Toilet paper holder spring." She grinned and shrugged.

His heart went wild and he framed her face. "If I didn't already madly love you, this would be the moment I fell hard for you."

As his lips met hers, Bridge's voice interrupted them. "We got the crybaby subdued. Tear gas. Nice touch. Cops are down the road."

He entered the room and turned his nose up at Harley Coburn's lifeless body. "Well, points for originality." He punched Libby in the arm. "You good, Warrior Princess?"

She rolled her eyes. "I am now." She leaned into Axel and wrapped her arms around his waist.

"Ah. Nice. Does this mean you're not leaving us for the second best protection agency in the world?"

Libby laughed. "Yes. And don't let Wilder Flynn hear you say that."

Bridge laughed as Amber rushed into the room. "Cops have Hunter Parks. Archer is on the phone with them. She glanced at Harley and then Macy. "Eew." Amber pushed Axel away and hugged Libby for herself. "Girl, you are bad to the bone."

"I actually took out Harley," Axel said.

"Gloater," Amber teased, and hugged Libby even tighter.

Once they gave their statements to the police

and the scene was turned over to the forensics and coroner, they walked outside into the spring breeze.

"I'd like to go to the hospital and be with Cass," Libby said.

"You got it." Axel paused at the car door and pulled her to him, kissing her until his insides turned to mush, and he couldn't care less if Amber and Bridge saw. He was a man so thoroughly and deeply in love he didn't know what to do with himself.

Well, he did. And if he had his way, they'd spend the rest of their lives together.

EPILOGUE

"Why are we at Bono's Gym?" Libby asked.

Two weeks had passed since they'd faced off with The Eye and won. Hunter had pinned everything on Harley, as if he'd made Hunter murder some of those women. The court could decide his fate and that was fine with Libby.

Cass was out of the hospital and healing. Libby had declined the job offer in Atlanta, and Wilder had been gracious. She was done making fear-based choices. Now, she was making faith-based decisions and loving Axel was one of them. She trusted God with both their lives, and she had faith Axel wouldn't behave recklessly because of his love for her. They were going to make a future together but hanging out at a gym wasn't on her list of things to do. She was still waiting on a ring to seal the deal for the days ahead.

Axel led her into the boxing ring of the gym, the smell of sweat, garlic, tomatoes and basil wafting on the air.

"Do I smell pizza?"

"Nonna's. I thought we'd have dinner after." He grinned. "I even brought extra ranch."

"I'm all ranched out these days," she teased. "And after what? Why are we at a boxing ring?"

"Well," he said nonchalantly, but mischief danced in his eyes, "you keep saying you can take me down."

She poked him in the chest. "And you keep saying I can't."

"I figure now's the time to put our money where our mouths are." He climbed into the ring, holding open the ropes for her to join him. "Gloves on or off?"

"You choose." She had no idea what he was up to. Did he really want to go a few rounds with her? She'd rather go a few rounds kissing.

Axel tossed her a set of boxing gloves and she donned them. Then he pulled a little black box from his pocket and opened it to reveal a gorgeous princess cut diamond.

She stood stunned and gasped.

"Loser proposes. Winner accepts." He placed the ring box with the sparkling diamond dead center of the ring. "Because, Libby, no matter what, we're getting married. It's all just semantics now."

She laughed. "And pride. And bragging rights." Her heart soared. Axel Spears wanted to marry her. The question was, did she want a traditional proposal with him on his knees or something more modern? Hmm... She did kinda want both: him proposing and her with bragging rights.

"Not sure how many couples kick the snot out of each other in order to propose but the way I figure, the couple who slays together stays together." Axel danced around the ring box using fancy footwork, but that wouldn't save him. "Give me your best, Libs. I got all night." He smacked his gloves together and raised them to his face.

Libby cackled and snorted, dancing around and keeping her fists in front of her face to protect it. "Oh Axel, as if it'll take me that long to put your butt on the floor. I want my ring, and the pizza before it goes cold."

Axel continued to bob and dance. "We'll see."

"Oh, we will."

She waited for him to take a jab, then dipped under his arm and went straight for the right kidney without an ounce of mercy. He grunted and dropped to his knees. "Remember the low blow you dealt me on day one in the conference room when you wanted me off the case? Just returning the favor."

His eyes watered as he peered up at her from his knees, unable to talk.

"And since you're out of breath, I'll save you the words and just say, yes!" Libby knelt and ripped off her boxing gloves.

"You crossed a line." His voice was strained.

"You didn't set one." She smirked and kissed him. "I want my ring now."

He chuckled and coughed then pulled off his gloves. He gently removed the ring from the velvet box, gliding it onto her ring finger. "Libby Winters, you wild and wonderful woman, will you marry me?"

"If you admit I did indeed take you down."

He laughed and drew her to him, his eyes widening. "You're wearing that perfume I liked."

"I didn't know where we were going, but it felt like it was going to be special. And I was right. As usual."

He leaned in and ran his nose along the side of her neck, landing below her ear where she'd dabbed it. "I liked it then. I really like it now," he whispered, sending chills along her ribs.

"Good. Now. Admit I took you down—and not by the perfume."

He chuckled against her ear then pulled away, longing and playfulness dancing in his eyes. "You already said yes."

Before she could protest, he claimed her lips, giving her a promise for a bright and unpredictable future, one that would never be boring or without banter.

So she didn't care if he admitted it or not. All she needed was him.

Forever.

* * * * *

*If you enjoyed this Elite Protectors book
by Jessica R. Patch,
be sure to read the
previous book in the series,*
Attempted Mountain Abduction,
available now from Love Inspired Suspense!

Dear Reader,

Sometimes trusting others, and God, is hard due to hard life experiences. It becomes easier to live in the fear of "What if?" than walk in faith and trust that God is always our comfort and even if bad things happen again, He is able to get us through with that same comfort and grace. It was pretty apparent from the start that Axel loved Libby, but her fear kept her paralyzed and navigated her choices. Choices she thought she had to make to protect herself. It took really seeing what her life might be like without Axel to turn it around and make the choice she knew she needed to make all along. It's easy to see someone else's fear-based choices and think they need to get over it and move forward. But it's a lot harder when it's our fear leading the charge. We need to be more gracious and we need to fully accept God's grace. Perfect love casts out all fear. I love to connect with readers. Join my Patched In monthly newsletter and receive a free short thriller at www.jessicarpatch.com.

Warmly,
Jessica

Get up to 4 Free Books!

We'll send you 2 free books from each series you try PLUS a free Mystery Gift.

FREE Value Over $25

Both the **Love Inspired®** and **Love Inspired® Suspense** series feature compelling novels filled with inspirational romance, faith, forgiveness and hope.

YES! Please send me 2 FREE novels from the Love Inspired or Love Inspired Suspense series and my FREE gift (gift is worth about $10 retail). After receiving them, if I don't wish to receive any more books, I can return the shipping statement marked "cancel." If I don't cancel, I will receive 6 brand-new Love Inspired Larger-Print books or Love Inspired Suspense Larger-Print books every month and be billed just $7.19 each in the U.S. or $7.99 each in Canada. That is a savings of 20% off the cover price. It's quite a bargain! Shipping and handling is just 50¢ per book in the U.S. and $1.25 per book in Canada.* I understand that accepting the 2 free books and gift places me under no obligation to buy anything. I can always return a shipment and cancel at any time by calling the number below. The free books and gift are mine to keep no matter what I decide.

Choose one:
- ☐ **Love Inspired Larger-Print** (122/322 BPA G36Y)
- ☐ **Love Inspired Suspense Larger-Print** (107/307 BPA G36Y)
- ☐ **Or Try Both!** (122/322 & 107/307 BPA G36Z)

Name (please print)

Address   Apt. #

City   State/Province   Zip/Postal Code

Email: Please check this box ☐ if you would like to receive newsletters and promotional emails from Harlequin Enterprises ULC and its affiliates. You can unsubscribe anytime.

Mail to the Harlequin Reader Service:
IN U.S.A.: P.O. Box 1341, Buffalo, NY 14240-8531
IN CANADA: P.O. Box 603, Fort Erie, Ontario L2A 5X3

Want to explore our other series or interested in ebooks? Visit www.ReaderService.com or call **1-800-873-8635**.

---

*Terms and prices subject to change without notice. Prices do not include sales taxes, which will be charged (if applicable) based on your state or country of residence. Canadian residents will be charged applicable taxes. Offer not valid in Quebec. This offer is limited to one order per household. Books received may not be as shown. Not valid for current subscribers to the Love Inspired or Love Inspired Suspense series. All orders subject to approval. Credit or debit balances in a customer's account(s) may be offset by any other outstanding balance owed by or to the customer. Please allow 4 to 6 weeks for delivery. Offer available while quantities last.

Your Privacy—Your information is being collected by Harlequin Enterprises ULC, operating as Harlequin Reader Service. For a complete summary of the information we collect, how we use this information and to whom it is disclosed, please visit our privacy notice located at https://corporate.harlequin.com/privacy-notice. Notice to California Residents – Under California law, you have specific rights to control and access your data. For more information on these rights and how to exercise them, visit https://corporate.harlequin.com/california-privacy. For additional information for residents of other U.S. states that provide their residents with certain rights with respect to personal data, visit https://corporate.harlequin.com/other-state-residents-privacy-rights/.

LIRLIS25